IMMORAL ORIGINS

THE DESIRE CARD BOOK ONE

LEE MATTHEW GOLDBERG

ROUGH
EDGES
PRESS

Immoral Origins
Paperback Edition
Copyright © 2022 Lee Matthew Goldberg

Rough Edges Press
An Imprint of Wolfpack Publishing
5130 S. Fort Apache Rd. 215-380
Las Vegas, NV 89148

roughedgespress.com

Paperback ISBN 978-1-68549-085-0
eBook ISBN 978-1-68549-084-3
LCCN 2022936758

IMMORAL ORIGINS

"Right is right even if no one is doing it; wrong is wrong even if everyone is doing it."

— **Saint Augustine**

PROLOGUE

THERE'S A GUN TO THE BACK OF MY HEAD.

The hammer makes a clicking sound, whoever it is ain't fucking around. I should've seen this coming. It's either the one I fear, or he's sent someone in his place because he's too gutless to do it himself. Fucking bastard. Had me strip away every shred of morals and left me a hollow cave. Over the years, the blood on my palms has seeped into my love lines, my life lines, my fate lines. I've visited the graves of those I'd put in the earth. I expect nothing less than a direct elevator to hell when this tormentor finally pulls the trigger. Maybe I've been waiting for it. Doing exactly the wrong thing in the hopes that I'll see the end. Because there's no escaping. That's what the Desire Card promises along with every wish it fulfills.

But it wasn't always supposed to be this way. Troublemaking kid from Hell's Kitchen— *sure*—but mostly petty crimes. Figuring out ways to steal from the rich and give to the poor (i.e. me). Yeah, I'd spent time behind bars, but baby bars, not maximum security.

Shoplifting something stupid. Drunk tank. Purse snatch. Drunk tank. Breaking and entering (they never proved that one). Maggs and I did it mostly because we were bored. I'd dropped out of high school and so did he. We flipped burgers at a smelly diner on Eighth Avenue but that paid shit. Then I was fired and Maggs quit out of loyalty because we'd done everything together since the sandbox. And my girl Cheryl wanted a diamond tennis bracelet because she heard some celebrity on TV yapping about her husband getting her one for their anniversary. I was already planning on dumping Cheryl because I'd heard she got with Crazy Eddie who fucked anything with limbs and might've given her the clap. But at the time, I'd seen this tennis bracelet in the window at Tiffany's and my god did it twinkle. I figured even if Cheryl didn't deserve it, my next girl would. So I tried to swipe it and SLAMMO— jail time number five. Maggs bailed me out with money he lifted from his mom and I moved back home with my folks and ailing little brother Emile who'd spent half of his life in hospitals. Ma yelled at me to take my GED and get a job. Pop tanned me with his belt. Emile cried. I went to sleep with the left side of my body all bruised and swore I'd figure out some way to wrench my life out of the pits I'd been in for too long.

And *voila*, on Halloween Night 1978, I was dressed like Robin Hood because he fit my motto and met Marilyn Monroe. A masked wonder who led me on the path of greatness before death came lurking. To this gun poking the back of my head. To my brains Jackson Pollocked on the wall.

But that night, I was simply star struck...

1978

1

So Cheryl was lying like the gypsies on my block who promised fortunes told.

Swore up and down she'd never been with Crazy Eddie and the clap was really a yeast infection. I wasn't buying it. My girl would twirl a curl every time she fudged the truth. Wrapping her white-blonde hair around a pink nail-polished finger and looking off in the distance like something far away caught her eye.

"I'm not even attracted to Crazy Eddie," she said, throwing up her arms. "He's got noodles for legs."

I could argue that multiple people saw them tonguing at the Two for One bar, but she was already going ballistic.

"Maybe you're accusing me because you were with Gina Constantine," she said. Gina, who had a lazy eye and a pronounced limp. I was offended by the association.

"Gina's been in the hospital," I said, which was true because she was getting her leg realigned.

"And how do you know that?"

I ignored her. I'd went back to Tiffany's and stolen the tennis bracelet right, then came over that Halloween night to invite her to this party Maggs heard about. Maggs was waiting downstairs so we could take the train. I wanted to be the bigger person, but Cheryl made that hard.

"The point is, Cheryl, *you're* the one who cheated and here *I*, good ol' me, came to give you a tennis bracelet, but you won't even admit to what you've done."

"A tennis bracelet?" she asked, rubbing her hands together and pouting her lips. Cheryl had a Cupid's face with big eyes that always seemed surprised, baby fat cheeks, and Farrah Fawcett hair like every damn girl on the block. She lowered the volume of "How Deep is Your Love" on the record player because she was actually interested in the conversation. She even had the nerve to hold out her wrist.

"I was gonna give it to you if you were honest."

She huffed. "I am!"

"I can smell Crazy Eddie's English Leather aftershave on you."

"That's ridiculous. You're ridiculous."

"*And* I was gonna invite you to this party—"

"A Disco party?"

She'd been obsessed with Disco since seeing *Saturday Night Fever*. I had to take her twice. I didn't see the fuss. With the movie or with Disco. John Travolta may have been a Casanova in Cheryl's mind but I thought he was a putz.

"It's a Halloween party."

"That explains the clothes."

"I'm Robin Hood."

"Aren't you a little old for dress-up?"

I took out the tennis bracelet just to see her get jealous. She nearly knocked me over to get at it.

"*Tiffany's?*"

I opened the box and then closed it as her grubby fingers reached for the shiny object.

"Jake!"

"Nuh-uh, you haven't fessed up."

She blew her bangs from her eyes. "Fine. Fine, Jake. Ok, I was smashed and ran into Crazy Eddie at the Two and One. Well, two and one led to four and two, which led to—"

"I get your point." I was already putting away the Tiffany's box.

"And you weren't around."

"Emile got sick again. Like, I've been taking care of my kid brother."

"You weren't in the drunk tank?"

"Maybe for one night but other than that I've been on sick brother duty. And Maggs and I ain't working at the Nedicks anymore so there's no money coming in."

She gestured blah, blah, blah with her hand like she'd heard it all before.

"So you lifted the bracelet?"

"Would you care if it was on your wrist?"

She rose one shoulder, slender and egg-shaped, resting her chin against the bone.

"I think it's time for you to go, Robin Hood."

When I got downstairs, Maggs was smoking his John Players, pinching the cigarette between his index finger and thumb like a mobster. His mustache flapped as he spat out the smoke and then ran his hand through his shaggy hair. I didn't have to tell him that Cheryl wasn't coming, a look said it all. He squeezed my shoulder, gave me a smoke, and we headed toward the 1 train because this party was way downtown.

In the train car, leaning our heads against the graffitied walls where someone tagged faloupoo in big block letters, trying not to listen to a group of teenage girls singing songs from *Grease*—I couldn't escape John Travolta—Maggs doing this trick where he puts a penny on the back of his hand and then *abracadabra* it's gone. It got me every time.

"But where does it go?"

Like I was a little kid, he reached behind my ear and *presto* the penny appeared.

"So you and Cheryl are Splittsville?"

"Yup," I said, chewing on a piece of Freshen-Up, the liquid center bursting and oozing down my throat.

"No girl, no job..." he said, shaking his head.

"Hey, you ain't such a good cheer up committee."

"This party may be the turnaround you need."

"Who's hosting again?"

"You know Jack, Jack Something-Or-Other. Jack with the nose, you know he's got that nose."

I didn't know.

"Jack, one of Georgie's guys."

Georgie. Some might call him a mobster. In Georgie's mind, he liked to think he was. Mostly he sold hot coats down by the FDR.

"I picked up some odd jobs from Georgie," Maggs said. "Just opening up the back doors of delivery vans while they're stopped in traffic and swiping the goods. Most don't lock 'em. Then he gives me a cut."

"Lemme guess, seventy-thirty in his favor."

Maggs got quiet. Bingo, I was right.

"Okay, okay," he said. "But it's money and I ain't choosey. What gigs do you have?"

"I spent my last twenty on this outfit."

Maggs eyed me up and down. "Not such a wise investment. If you want, I'll put a good word in with Georgie."

It wasn't that I was against working for a so-called mobster like Georgie. Ethically, I mean. Rather I wanted a cut better than thirty percent. Emile's medical bills were reaching the five figures.

"We'll talk to Jack at the party and figure it out from there," Maggs said, before jumping up and joining the gaggle of girls by singing "You're the One that I Want" in a high falsetto. The girls flipped their hair and pretended not to care, but I could tell they liked Maggs because everyone did. He flexed a muscle at them, then switched to the other arm, back and forth until they finally giggled. When we were three, our mothers left us in a sandbox and Maggs whacked me with a Tonka Truck. He split my head open and I needed stitches and our moms went apeshit. After the doctor's visit, Maggs's ma invited us over where we ate ambrosia salad and watched fucking Howdy Doody because they had the only television on the block. We'd been friends ever since.

He whipped out a penny and the girls *ooohhhed* and *ahhhhed* as he made it vanish and then produced a penny from behind each of their tiny ears.

"Hey, you ain't making enough to be giving those pennies away," I said. The girls giggled more but the train slowed at Chambers Street and Maggs realized it was our stop so he grabbed me by the collar and pulled me onto the platform. The girls gave peace signs through the window before they disappeared into the tunnel. Maggs opened up his palm revealing a stack of pennies.

"But how did you...?"

"A magician never reveals their trick," Maggs said, with a smile that only showed his bottom teeth because his mustache was so damn bushy.

THE TWIN TOWERS, MAJESTIC ALONG THE HORIZON, bringing a halt to the decline of lower manhattan.

I'd heard my pop speak of them this way. The tallest buildings in the world until the Sears Tower went up in '73. Built at a time when New York's future seemed uncertain, the towers restored confidence. The Empire State sturdy like a man, the Chrysler sexy like a woman, the towers a show of incomparable mystique. That loony French dude walked a high-wire between them a few years back. The Human Fly hoisted himself up the south tower. I'd planned on taking Cheryl to Windows on the World for our anniversary, but now I'd need to find a new girl to show-off the sights. Seeing the skyline reflecting them on Halloween night, I thought that anything could be possible. Money for Emile's surgeries, really falling in love, moving out of my folks', finding a job worthwhile of sinking my teeth into.

Downtown resembled a wasteland so I was surprised when we entered a factory-like space. Turns out, Jack with the Nose's uncle owned a toy distributor and let Jack have the place for a soiree. Andy Gibb's "Shadow Dancing" pumped from out of the doors once they swung open. Packed house. Wonder Womans, Sandra Dees, Debbie Harrys, Chewbaccas, Andy Warhols, New York Yankees who just won the 75th World Series, John Belushi from *Animal House*, Mork from *Mork and Mindy* (Nanoo nanoo!), two Coneheads, a Superman, a Sid & Nancy couple, and about eight warring guys strutting around as John Travolta. Maggs said he was dressed as an undercover cop, which really meant he was too lazy to come up with a costume. "Can you dig it," he'd say to anyone who asked.

"Far out," a few replied.

"Keep your enemies close, right?" Maggs said, and everyone agreed cops were bogus.

"Who are you?" a Chrissy from *Three's Company* asked.

"Robin Hood."

"Robin Byrd?"

She was on so much coke, it had crusted around her nostrils.

"Hood. Robin Hood."

She tapped her temple in deep thought. "What have I seen him in?"

"Your nightmares," I said, fucking with her but then she began to cry. Maggs rubbed her shoulder and led her away.

"Don't scare the lovelies," he said.

Jack with the Nose approached. I knew it was him, since his nose was really a sight. Not simply big, it had a presence, elbowing its way into conversations, bulbous and red like an old drunk's, a whistle escaping from his nostrils every time he spoke.

"Jack, you know Jake," Maggs said. "He's looking for work."

"Really, really?" Jack with the Nose asked. He was wearing a big purple pimp coat with a walking stick and large tinted sunglasses. "I work for Georgie."

"I've met Georgie."

"Yeah, how good are you at nabbing coats?"

"That's very specific."

"We're...uh...a *specific* kind of organization."

"I just stole a Tiffany's bracelet for my ex-girl."

"Coats are a lot bigger," Jack with the Nose said, and popped a cigarette between his lips.

"But do they have diamonds?"

"Come down to the Fish Market at the Seaport tomorrow night, you can talk to Georgie there. We'll find something for ya."

"Thanks, Jack, that's real nice of you," Maggs said.

Jack with the Nose brushed it off like it was no big deal, but it was clear he wanted adulation.

"Yeah, real nice," I managed to say.

"Go," Jack with the Nose ordered. "Mingle. Make some new friends. That Marilyn's been eye fucking ya."

He pointed his cigarette through the throngs of the party, past a heap of sloshed dancers feeling each other up, to where a Marilyn Monroe in her iconic white dress was having a difficult time keeping it from billowing up, yet there was no wind tunnel under her feet.

Clearly eye-fucking me unless she had a nervous tic, I knocked back a vodka shot being passed around and made my way over. She wore a mask, not of the plastic variety like a Halloween kid's costume, but as if it had actually molded into her face. The hair was her own, styled perfectly, the color of sunrays. A vampy sway accompanied her movements as she danced to "Kiss You All Over" by Exile.

Oh baby wanna taste your lips, wanna be your fantasy.

Did she know that over my bed hung a poster of Marilyn Monroe from *Gentlemen Prefer Blondes*? That I'd seen *Some Like It Hot* every time it was rereleased in the theaters. I didn't get along with my parents for the most part, but we had a love for movies in common. Maybe because you can go to a movie with people you normally argue with and no one has to speak. Maybe because movies seemed to calm Emile's fits when nothing else did. Restaurants were a no-no (he tended to throw food), but plant him in front of a big screen with a popcorn in his lap and the kid would go numb. For my folks, it gave them two hours off. Marilyn Monroe, man, I was a pipsqueak when she died, so sad. But movie stars, they get to live on. Immortality at its finest. And at that Halloween party, she'd been resurrected for me, mouthing the words to "Kiss You All Over".

A whoosh of hot air pushed me towards her and we danced before we even spoke. Marilyn Monroe doing The Hustle, The Bump, The Bus Stop and The Lawnmower really a sight. I tried to keep up, but Disco ain't my thing. Give me the Stones, the Beatles, Springsteen, and always Led Zeppelin. My door locked, a pair of Koss Pro4AAs headphones, and "Houses of the Holy" spinning on my record player, a good joint to kick in around "The Rain Song". But this Marilyn clearly loved

"Stayin' Alive" so I aped all the strutting John Travoltas at the party so she'd keep on eye-fucking me.

"I'm so hot," she finally said, and I agreed she was hot but then she fanned her flush mask and I realized she meant it was hot in here. "There's a roof." She pointed up to the ceiling as if I'd never heard of a roof before and laced her fingers in mine. We ascended a twisty staircase and popped up two stories higher on a roof with no guardrails. The Hudson River behind us, the World Trade Center at our feet like I could reach out and touch the towers. The downtown quiet and restless. The future held a much different outcome for it than how it appeared then.

"I'm a genie in a bottle," she said, in her cutesy voice, an exact replica of the screen legend.

Under us, "Stayin' Alive" boomed. I randomly pictured someone stabbed in the back, crawling to get away from their pursuer. My mind went weird like that sometimes.

"Oh yeah?" I laughed. "What wishes can you grant?"

She stopped swaying to the beats, dead serious. "Any wish fulfilled...for the right price. Aren't you tired of stealing from the rich to only give to the poor?"

I beamed. "You get my costume."

She took small steps toward the edge, peered down three stories. "Now I'm cold," she said. "I can't win."

"Here." I removed my Robin Hood jacket and draped it around her arms.

"So gallant."

I didn't know what that meant, but I imagined it a compliment.

"Who do you know at the party?" I asked.

"No one. I was passing by, heard music, and wandered inside."

"What were you doing down here?" In my knowledge, nobody came to Tribeca at night, maybe a prostitute or two, but it was pretty lifeless otherwise.

"Seeking a party like this and a kind of thief like you."

She tapped my nose with her long fingernail and smiled. I could see it vaguely growing under her mask.

"Why Marilyn?"

She thought about this for some time, as if she wanted to get the answer right.

"She's two personas, Norma Jean and Marilyn. Kinda like me. Kinda like everyone. The self we keep hidden and the one we reveal to the world."

"Very poetic."

"I work for a company that encourages this dualistic nature."

She lost me. Big words and such. The problem from never finishing high school. I must have looked confused because she continued by saying, "My boss believes we have these two sides. One deals with our traumatic pasts and we all have traumatic pasts, believe me. But you don't always have to wallow in that sadness, you can be free."

"Sounds very Hare Krishna."

"It's not religious at all. It's about business. We fulfill wishes."

"Any wishes?"

"For the right price, remember? What do you wish for?"

I wanted to tell her about Emile and all the surgeries he needed. That my pop was working two jobs and even my ma was doing some side hustle to make bread. That I gave them a cut of everything I stole and resold, even though they were kind of chumps. My pop had opportunities he passed on because he didn't find them kosher. There was a Georgie-type on our block who had even more lucrative jobs he offered my pop years ago but Pop turned him down because he didn't "like that racket" and made sure I'd never do work for the guy either. Pop was a fool. He could've had all the money he needed for Emile's surgeries and likely would've avoided jail, but he was too high and mighty. He puffed out his chest, declared himself "good", and the conversation was closed. So if I could really wish for anything, it'd be for him not to be a dupe.

I shuffled a lone Lucky Strike out of my front pocket and lit up. Filling my lungs and getting that queasy sensation I'd dreamed about all day.

"I'm stuck, ya-know," I said, like she was my therapist. A real face didn't stare back, only this frozen expression of a mask. I zeroed on her lovely rubber birthmark.

"You want more," she purred. "Yes, yes."

"Yes, I...I dunno. It's like I'm living, but I am really living?"

"You're not," she said, swiping the cigarette from out of my mouth and placing it in the hole where her lips were visible. "I can see that all over you. No job, right?"

I wanted the cigarette back, but was afraid to try. "I might be getting work from this guy Georgie..."

"Fish," she said. "That's a lot of nothing. That guy with the nose you were talking to, he's a lot of nothing. Small fish."

"And I'm guessing who you work for is a tuna?"

Her dead eyes stared back.

"A tuna? Like a big fish? I was trying to be–"

"I get it." She tossed the cigarette and put it out with her toe. "He's an up-and-coming fish, let's put it that way. And he'd like your whole..." She drew an imaginary circle around me. "Milieu. The steal from the rich and give to poor bit we'll have to work on, though."

"So who do you grant these wishes to?"

"Those who line our pockets. You can take from the rich, charge a fee as long as you give something else back to them. Banks do it all the time. Anyway..." She glanced again over the ledge, leaning close enough that I thought she might jump, the backdrop of the Twin Towers framing her beautiful aura. I held her arm.

"Oh sweetie, I ain't about self-sabotage," she said. "I could've killed myself a long time ago when I was really down in the dumps, but the Jiminy Cricket on my shoulder told me to hang on because something bigger waited on the horizon. He was oh so right."

It was she who took hold of my arm then. Her touch frosty like she'd dipped her fingers in a bowl of ice.

"Let me take you away from here," she said. "Let me show you what you're missing, Robin Hood."

"It's Jake. Jake Barnum."

"Nice to meet you, Jake Barnum. I'm Marilyn Monroe."

I cocked my head to the side. She laughed.

"What's in a name?" she asked. "Your parents saw your birthed form and dubbed you Jake. They didn't know you yet. They just assumed. It's more powerful to name yourself."

"So what should I be called?"

"You're a *long* way from that accomplishment. But I have a feeling I know who you'll be."

"And who is that?"

"Why, Robin Hood himself. Mr. Errol Flynn."

3

MARILYN MONROE CONVINCED ME TO LEAVE THE party.

I got a thumbs up from Maggs on my way out, clearly agreeing I'd scored good talent. He was left floundering with Chrissy from *Three's Company*. Marilyn yanked me past the faux Travoltas like she had a mission to get me far away from this sham. Outside, the low buildings created a wind tunnel and Marilyn had to keep patting her skirt down.

"Let's just walk," she said. "Towards the Village. And go to an all-night diner."

"Sounds like a plan."

We strolled along the west side, arm-in-arm. She was quiet so I filled the silences. How I grew up in Hell's Kitchen. That my father was a garbage man and often brought home precious finds from along his route. Some nights he drove a livery cab too. My ma worked part-time as a legal secretary. It was a trade-off for her to leave the house because she had to find someone to watch Emile. Sometimes her neighbor Dolores did it, since the woman lost her husband and was home all the time crocheting. Ma would pay her by baking muffins or some shit like that. But she didn't want to be away from Emile for too long because it made him upset.

Usually when I mentioned Emile, people wanted to know more about his issues. The problem being we didn't exactly know. The amount of doctors who scratched their heads too many to count. He had mental issues, the least of our worries. He also had cerebral palsy. And something was wrong with his guts. At times, he was able to digest foods but a lot he couldn't take. So he stayed frighteningly skinny. His wheelchair had broken so we were in the process of getting him a new one. I was debating selling the bracelet I'd pilfered to help.

"You do a lot for him," she said, the first she had spoken in a while. She had been so quiet I wasn't sure she was really listening. Especially since the mask covered up any facial reactions.

"He's my kid brother, the only one I have. Someone's got to protect him. One day my folks won't be around anymore and it'll all be left up to me."

My words floated in the air, waiting for her to acknowledge them. She was like a robot in that sense, devoid of human characteristics. All the girls I'd been with had been fiery and difficult, never silent and hidden. I wanted to know everything about her.

Me: Have you always lived in New York?
Her: No.
Me: Can you take off the mask?

Her: NO.
Me: Why?
Her: ....

We reached the West Village and she said how much she loved the Waverly Diner where your omelet arrives still in the frying pan. No one looked twice at her with the mask since it was still Halloween, although all the other patrons' costumes were in various stages of disarray.

"Can you eat with it on?" I asked, trying to be funny.

"I can do *everything* with it on," she said, and gave a wink through the eye hole.

We ordered Greek omelets, and sure enough, they came delivered to our table still in a frying pan. She ate hers with the zeal of a ravenous shark, devouring it to pieces while I only managed two bites.

"Are you for real?" I asked.

She scooped up my hands. "I want to get out of here. I want you to meet someone."

"Who?"

"My boss." She flagged down a waiter and asked for a cigarette and the check. He lit one for her and she puffed away.

"I think you might want to join our organization." Puff. "There's a trial period of course." Longer puff. "Before you get a mask of course." She blew a smoke ring that haloed my head.

"A mask? So you wear those at work? Are you working now?"

"I'm always working," she said, as if it were both a tragedy and a source of pride.

The waiter brought over the check.

"What are the masks for?"

"In-cog-nito," she said, between smoke breaths. "The kind of work I do, we can't have the clients knowing our true faces. Insurance wise."

"O-*kay*."

"My boss will explain it a lot better."

I checked my watch. It was after midnight.

"Your boss is working now?"

"Like I said," she said, stubbing out her cigarette. "*Always* working. Finish your eggs."

I went to take a bite but she had already thrust herself out of the booth, her high heels clomping out of the diner. I took a big bite and followed. When I stepped outside, I didn't see her. The streets far from empty so I looked to make sure she wasn't blocked by the throngs of dwellers pouring out of the bars. But she had vanished like I'd conjured her out of my imagination. I wondered for a second if the vodka shot I drank had been laced.

"Jake," a voice peeped from behind me. Marilyn was adjusting her mask. Apparently, it had become askew. "Is it straight?" she asked, full of fear that it could be anything less than ideal.

I placed my hands on her cheeks—well, the mask's cheeks—which felt rather real. Not rubbery or plastic. Smooth.

"Wow," I said. "No, you're perfect."

She kissed me through the mouth hole and I had to awkwardly swallow the last bit of omelet. Her tongue poked through like a submarine torpedo, exploding against my back molars. Passerby hooted and hollered as I dipped her in my arms. She pulled away, flush, and threw her hand into the air to hail a cab. One stopped as she got inside, her legs dangling onto the curb. Beckoning me to come inside, into her world, her private wonder.

4

THE BOSS'S OFFICE WAS SMACK IN THE MIDDLE OF midtown, Park Avenue and 47th Street to be exact.

The kind of building that rose for about fifty stories near the Helmsley Hotel. After getting in an elevator where we needed a key, we went to the second floor and turned down a long hallway with a door at the end. Inside the lights were kept low, a masked receptionist banging away at a typewriter. The receptionist had a 100s cigarette in her lips, the smoke escaping upwards and getting tossed around by a whirling ceiling fan. She had brown hair, thick eyebrows, powerful cheekbones. But it was her eyes I noticed the most: a swelling of the muscles and surrounding tissues that pushed them forward through the holes in the mask.

"This is Bette," Marilyn said, stifling a yawn.

"Oh right," I said. "Bette Davis. Sure."

Bette Davis gave me a look that said: *Dumbass*.

"Is the boss in for company?" Marilyn asked.

Bette Davis kept banging away, doing serious

damage to the typewriter. She ripped out the piece of paper and placed in another.

"He's in," she mumbled, through her cigarette.

"Well, can you buzz him?"

This was delivered with a heavy heaping of sass. These women did not like each other. Bette stared down Marilyn who gave her the same glare back, neither wanting to be the one to flinch.

Finally, World War III ended with Bette pushing a button on the intercom.

"Marilyn to see you." Her thick eyebrows rose towards me like two curious caterpillars.

"Uh, Jake Barnum," I said, nervous for some reason. I wasn't sure why, usually nothing made me flinch. But this tiny office with its remnants of a bygone era: wood walls, low orange furniture, brown carpeting and palm plants galore. Like I'd stepped into a frozen time capsule between the décor and the two old movie sirens.

Bette pushed the intercom button. "And a Jake Barnum."

She hadn't put out her cigarette yet and the ash hung on like a stubborn worm.

Buzz. "Send them in," came the reply from the intercom.

Bette waved us away toward a door and then went right back to pummeling the typewriter.

"What's she writing?" I whispered to Marilyn once we were out of earshot.

"I dunno. She's *loco en la cabeza*."

Marilyn rapped two knocks and opened the door to my new destiny.

Inside, all class. A wet bar in a corner with top shelf

liquor I'd never even tried. Red walls, backlit, with a golden pig by the mahogany desk.

"It brings good luck," the boss said, patting the pig's head. He wore a mask too, easily identifiable. Clark Gable. The mustache seeming like it was made from real hairs. "Actually, a client had requested it. Was made during the Han Dynasty. Only two in the world. I liked it so much I purchased the other one. Gable, here."

He put out his hand and shook mine before I had a chance to speak. His grip strong and assured. I gave him the same squeeze as we crunched each other's finger bones.

"Jake Barnum."

"My receptionist Bette said. And you've met Marilyn."

Marilyn curtsied.

"She doesn't bring home just anyone, strays I mean. We seek only those who can offer value. Please, sit."

He pointed to a great leather chair, worn like a catcher's glove. It swallowed me up as I sat. He and Marilyn found their places behind the desk. We were interviewing each other. I was intrigued: by Marilyn, by their whole show. Clearly these people made loads of money, despite their weird behaviors.

"So Marilyn tells me you fulfill wishes?"

Both of them gave a firm nod.

"I'll tell you our origin," Gable said. "My partner and I, Laurence Olivier, we had a wine business. Lucrative but small potatoes. We had a client who wanted a Chateaux Margaux 1787, goes for almost a hundred thousand dollars, and we procured it, our biggest find yet. I thought, why limit ourselves to only grape pleasures?"

Marilyn laughed so loud I felt a twitch in my neck. She fawned over Gable, tittering away.

"So now if it's sought after, if it's so desired, we will find it. As you can imagine, we have very high-profile clients."

"And the masks keep you incognito?"

Gable tapped his nose, a gesture it seemed like he did often.

"Whenever you're dealing with the massively rich, you must be careful. These kind of people can buy and sell us, Jake. That's the nature of this world. They hold power and the things they seek are not always legal, as you can imagine."

"I...didn't."

"Well, think about it. If you had more money than you knew what to do with, what would you desire? We *want* what we cannot have. There lies the ethical slide we find ourselves on. But why should one deny themselves what has been deemed wrong by society? Different cultures have different laws. And even for those who believe we are judged by the almighty, religions can't agree on a god so there is none. Simple as that. I'm guessing you're Catholic."

"Uh yeah, how did–"

"You have an Irish look to you, black Irish."

"My ma's side, she came here from Cork when she was around my age."

Gable went to the bar and poured three glasses of Irish. He moved so swiftly, in command of his surroundings.

"But you don't subscribe to the dogma?"

I had no clue what he meant. My face did this thing when I was confused. My nose would pinch and I'd get these lines between my eyes.

"The faith, Jake, the tall tales."

"My folks go to church every Sunday, but it's been a while for me. They like to pray for my–"

I stopped, not wanting to give him a sob story.

"Your brother, Jake?" Marilyn asked.

"Yeah," I said, twiddling my thumbs.

"That's a shame, a real shame," Gable said, his hand on my shoulder kneading a knot.

"Like he needs a wheelchair, trying to get him that."

"What do you do for work?" Gable asked.

"Kinda in between gigs right now. And Marilyn said..."

"Yes, we don't bring in strays often. Highly intense vetting process as you can imagine."

"Who does he remind you of?" Marilyn asked. "Look what he's wearing."

Gable studied me, his pupils going wide and then small. "Ah yes, I see it."

"Errol Flynn," they said at the same time, and I got a shiver up my back.

"I'll tell you what I can do," Gable said. "A mini assignment, test the waters. For you and for us. Whether this is a fit."

"Yeah, sure, man, whatever you have."

"How about a delivery?"

Marilyn clapped her hands. "Yes," she said. "He'd be perfect for that."

Gable went to a cabinet and plucked out a tiny blue box with a bow. He placed it in my hands. Despite its size, it felt heavy.

"What is it?"

Gable shook his finger. "Not for you to ask. Only to deliver. Here's the address."

"Now?"

"No time like the present. The client is waiting."

"What about my face?"

"Yes, I see the dilemma, no mask. Let me see what I can find."

He opened the door to a closet. I could see a few masks lined up. Joan Crawford, Gregory Peck, Spencer Tracy, I recognized them all.

"I don't have an Errol Flynn," he said. "Nor are you ready to earn a permanent mask. But this..."

He took a faceless one out. It had hair and holes for eyes, nose and a mouth, but the rest of the features hadn't been finished.

"I haven't decided on this creation yet," he said. "Put it on."

I did what he said. The mask's consistency was rubbery but very thin. It formed my face, clung onto pores, a second skin. Gable and Marilyn clearly approved with their giant grins. The address in my hand said 878 Park Ave, Theodora Birch.

He handed me another card.

"And to contact us once it's delivered."

THE DESIRE CARD

Any wish fulfilled for the right price.

Call to inquire.

(212) 555-CARD

Gable knocked back his drink and clapped his hands. This was clearly a signal for us to leave because

Marilyn cleaned up our whiskey glasses and took my arm toward the door.

"Thank you for this opportunity, Mr. Gable," I said. "I won't let you down."

It took a moment for him to answer. Made this sucking sound with his throat.

"Yes, I hope so. *Adieu*."

He gave a salute and then turned towards his massive windows. Through the reflection, he watched, scrutinized. I saluted back like a doofus and Marilyn whisked me out.

Her fingernails dug into my arm.

"He likes you," she said.

"Oh yeah?"

"He hates most everyone. So you're already ahead of the game."

5

I THOUGHT MARILYN MONROE WOULD JOIN ME FOR the job, but she said she needed to go to bed.

Gable gave me cab money and I whisked uptown in minutes. Being after three in the morning, a hazy light filtered down Park Avenue. A cold sun bubbling. Theodora Birch sure had fancy digs. Grand awning, a building that touched the clouds, and a doorman with white gloves. I put on the mask before entering and the doorman chuckled that it was still Halloween before he buzzed me up.

In the elevator, I shook the small blue box. Could hear a rattling noise, metal against cardboard, or a crinkling sound like from foil. The elevator reached the Penthouse and let out onto a hallway with old paintings that made it seem like a gallery at the Met. I rang Theodora Birch's doorbell and she opened up before it fully chimed.

She was a round woman. All cheeks and a floral muumuu. Her hair done up in a bun and held together by chopsticks, her feet wedged into slippers with a poof of feathers covering the toes. She could be thirty or fifty, hard to tell. Peering out in the hallway, she looked both ways before yanking me inside.

I'd never been in an apartment like hers before. Grand sweeping piano. Art all over like in the hallway outside. The walls painted forest green. Lacquered wooden floors except for a polar bear rug, the dead animal in mid-growl.

"Cordial?" she asked, and when I replied with my confused pinched face, she tapped her empty glass with the diamond ring on her finger. "It's a drink," she said, her frown enlarging. She proceeded to pour two glasses full of red liquor and handed me one with a gesture to sip. It tasted like sugared asshole, or at least as much as I was able to get down through the slit in the mask.

"Yum," I said, raising the glass for a cheers.

She fell gracefully onto a couch, tucking her legs under her butt with a pose.

"My wish?" she asked, her cheeks turning even more rosy.

"Of course." I placed the sweet drink down and procured the blue box from my pocket.

She clapped her hands and grabbed it fast. Opened the box with a pleasant smile. As she was about to remove the top, she realized I was still there.

"Privacy, please," she said, shooing me away. I turned around and heard a squeal similar to a squirrel getting its tail stepped on. Another squeal echoed and I looked over my shoulder to watch her pin a brooch on her large breast.

"You can turn around now," she said, displaying her prize, a pink diamond so bright it nearly blinded me.

"Very pretty, ma'am."

"Ma'am? No, that's for my mother. We're peers. It seems a little off-balance, no?"

She thrust her breast in my face, eyeing for me to fix. I carefully centered the brooch while not touching flesh.

"Rare, I assume?"

Her chins bounced. "Oh, very. Blood."

"What's that?"

"Blood diamond, the best. The only kind I wear. Anything else is too provincial."

"I've always said that."

A booming laugh devolved into a series of coughs that she eased with another sip of cordial.

"You must be hot with that mask on?" she asked. "Rather unspecific."

"I'm in training."

She nodded once, half-interested, still in awe of her brooch.

"Wanna know how much it cost?"

"I'm guessing a lot."

"A lot a lot. The pink ones come only from Sierra Leone. Sure, a warlord might've profited but who I am to say his cause is wrong? It's so far away. Another world."

"You don't have to justify."

Her frown grew longer, practically melting off her face.

"I know I don't."

"I'm only the messenger."

She finished her cordial in one gulp. "You haven't told me how beautiful I look."

"Oh? Yeah? Sure. It looks beautiful."

"*It* looks beautiful? Or *I* look beautiful?"

"It...you...both. Amazing really."

She eyed me waiting for a flinch. Heavily mascaraed, her lashes stuck together with each blink.

"Tell Clark Gable he's a genius."

With a stifled yawn, she waved me away like a peasant. Fucking rich people. All the same. Use and abuse. Put an apple in her mouth and she'd be no different than a pig at a roast, blood diamond or no blood diamond.

"Your drink tastes like shit," I said, swiveling around for the door, not seeing her reaction. Probably she gasped. I left, took the elevator down, and stopped at a phone booth to call the Desire Card. They picked up after the first ring.

"What is it that you wish for?" a voice asked. I recognized it as Bette's.

"It's Jake. Barnum. I made the delivery."

"Thank you."

Click.

"Hello?" A dial tone buzzed on the other line so I hung up and walked back to my parents' house. It was nearly dawn when I arrived, Hell's Kitchen with the odor of a sewer. Trash on the sidewalks, a far cry from snooty Park Avenue.

I lumbered up the three stories, hoping my folks hadn't woken yet because I needed sleep way more than a conversation. I could hear Emile whining from his room. He often didn't sleep, just moaned through the night. I had to turn on the fan usually to drown him out. Entering my room, the first thing I saw was the Marilyn Monroe poster over my bed. What a crazy night it had been, almost like a wild dream. I wondered if after I closed my eyes, I'd wake up with none of it ever happening at all.

6

Now I knew what they meant by sleeping like the dead.

Didn't get up once, not to pee, not until I heard arguing from the living room. A door slammed. I fought back a stiffy rooting around in my boxers, threw on some old jeans, and made my way out of the bedroom where a brand-new wheelchair waited by the front door. Pop and my ma hovered over it with looks of anger and delight. Emile drooled in the corner.

"What's this, Jake?" they both asked. Pop low and menacing, Ma shrill with a hint of Irish brogue.

"Looks like a wheelchair," I said, giving in to a yawning fit.

"There's a card," Pop said, still in his garbage man's uniform. Meaning it was around five in the afternoon before he switched over to his second job. Ma was in a blouse and stockings, probably having finished work too. "Says 'Glad to have you aboard' and is signed, Gable?"

I took the card. How did Gable even know where I

lived? At least he must've been satisfied with the delivery, despite my offending Theodora Birch.

"Who's Gable?" Ma asked.

"A new boss," I said, although the word felt funny in my mouth. There'd been no agreement I'd work for Gable. We were simply trying things out. But this wheelchair couldn't have come cheap.

"And he bought you a wheelchair?" Ma screamed. "Louie," she said to Pop. "Louie, can you believe this?"

"You're not working for Dick Mancini, are you?" Pop asked.

Dick Mancini being the so-called mobster on our block who wanted Pop to work for him for years. There was an unsaid agreement between the two that he'd never try to recruit me. Dick Mancini's gang good at stealing cars, even rubbing out rivals. He paid his boys well, but most had seen the inside of a prison.

"No, Pop, I told you I'd never take Dick Mancini's offers."

"This sure looks like something Dick Mancini would give for signing on. But it didn't come free."

"No, it's this guy Georgie," I said, regretting the lie even after it left my lips. "Maggs got me the work."

"Maggs," Pop and Ma huffed, neither too impressed by Maggs ever since he was four.

"Just deliveries, and I told him I wanted to be paid in a wheelchair for Emile."

I pointed at Emile so everyone would fucking understand the good news. Emile got a new wheelchair! The last one had a bum wheel that always skewed left. Also, the seat was worn. Emile laughed and clapped upon mention of his name. I went over and hugged the kid.

"See, Emile's happy. This is good news."

Pop touched his waist in reaching distance of his belt in case I needed a whooping.

"Well, thank you, Jakey," Ma finally said, leaving a kiss on my cheek and shuffling off into the kitchen humming, *Jack the jolly ploughboy*.

Pop wasn't entirely convinced.

"Don't do anything that'll get ya in over your head," he said. "Owing people money."

"I don't owe anyone nothing."

He slapped my cheek lightly, almost lovingly. "All right then Jakey, *grazie*. I gotta change, I smell like fish guts."

The fish market!

I was supposed to meet Georgie later that night. Luckily, I hadn't slept too much longer. My watch said six o' clock and working for Georgie would be a good cover to keep my folks from knowing the real job I was planning on taking.

"In fact, I gotta meet Georgie right now for another job downtown," I said.

Pop nodded, too exhausted to continue the interrogation. His eyes hung low, his five o' clock shadow had just hit midnight, and his shoulders slumped forward at such an angle I imagined his back was in knots. He worked and worked for this family, and even though I thought him a fool sometimes, he was a noble fool.

When I got down to the Seaport, I was hit with the sharp smell of decay. Night had fallen while tourists took their kids onto the docked boats. I spied Jack with the Nose, easy to notice in a crowd. He waved me over.

"Good timing," he said. "Jake, right? Lemme introduce you to Georgie."

I'd met Georgie before, but nodded so I wouldn't seem like an ass.

We went past the Fish Market and waited by the waters. A Circle Line cruise was headed toward the Statue of Liberty.

"I'd do her," Jack with the Nose said, indicating Lady Liberty.

"It would be an honor," I said, rolling along.

When Georgie appeared, I'd forgotten how short the guy was. 5'5 at the most, slicked-back hair starting to thin, a fur coat that seemed to wear him, sunglasses in the dark.

"This is Jake–" Jack with the Nose started to say.

"Of course I know Jake," Georgie said, reaching up to wrap his arm around my neck. "We go way back. Cigar?"

"Sure."

He lit cigars for me and Jack with the Nose. I hadn't smoked one in a while and forgot you weren't supposed to inhale.

"Whoa, don't die on us," Georgie said.

After a few embarrassing coughs, I got my shit together. "So Maggs said you might have work?"

"Jack filled me in," Georgie said. "Said you had some talented fingers for thieving."

"I like to think so."

"We can do a coat run."

"Yeah, sure."

"You know what that is?"

"Steal some coats?"

"There's an art to it, my friend. Right now, the department stores are getting their deliveries. We'll wait outside the loading docks of Gimbels."

"Sounds like something I can do."

We finished our cigars and Jack with the Nose drove us to midtown: Georgie sitting shotgun and me sliding from side-to-side in the back from Jack with the Nose's crazy driving. We parked and Georgie pointed at a truck about to back-up into a garage.

"Go and tell the driver you got the delivery covered," Georgie said. "Quick, before he goes inside."

"What about the workers?" I asked.

"We'll take care of the workers."

I hopped out and knocked on the truck driver's window. Made it as believable as possible for him to open the back right there. Pulled out of my ass that someone lit a stink bomb in the garage and we didn't want the merchandise to smell. Stupid driver bought it.

While I was removing two racks of coats hung from poles, I could see Georgie laughing with the workers inside the garage. Georgie was making them double over with laughter. Tears streamed from their eyes. He caught me looking at them and put a finger to his lips. I wheeled the racks over to where Jack with the Nose had parked, then stuffed the clothes inside. I went back over to the driver and told him thanks. Watched him drive away clueless. I wedged in with the coats while Georgie slid in shotgun and we roared off while "Hot Child in the City" cranked from the radio. We headed back to Georgie's spot by the FDR. By then, it was late enough that the tourists had mostly left. Besides the fishermen, the area turned seedy fast. A circle of men waited blowing into their hands from the cold off the water. We removed the coats and I watched a bidding war erupt. Coats selling for forty or fifty bucks, a steal for them but for us as well since it didn't cost a dime.

After about a half an hour, we'd moved the entire product.

"Good work there," Georgie said, handing me a hundred dollars.

"Wait, I think my cut's more than that. You probably made about a thousand."

"So?"

"So, Maggs said he gets like thirty percent."

"Maggs has been working for me for a while. This is your first run. We can negotiate after a few more."

I wanted to tell him to go fuck himself, but Jack with the Nose cracked his knuckles like he was ready to fight for Georgie's honor. So I shoved the money in my pocket and kept my mouth shut.

"We'll be in touch when there's more work," Jack with the Nose said.

I walked along the water breathing in the salt fumes. Sure I had a hundred bucks, but for the way I'd put my neck on the line, it should've been much more. I took out the Desire Card, mostly wanting to see Marilyn and realizing I'd never gotten her actual number.

"What is it you desire?" Bette asked, after a ring.

"It's Jake. Barnum."

Silence on the other end.

"Is Marilyn there?"

She sighed for what seemed like three hours.

"Hello?" a different voice asked. Marilyn the Sweet.

"Hey, it's me. It's Jake. I wanted to...well...thank Gable for the wheelchair."

"It's nothing."

"And that I'm real interested in more work. Like, I'm in, this is what I want to do."

"Uh-huh."

"And you, I'd like to see you again. Did you sleep well?"

"Two cats outside of my window were fucking all night," she said. "You know that a cat's penis is like a razor and it hurts the girl cat so that's why she makes such crazy sounds."

"I did not know that."

"But I had some nose candy and I'm wired. Let's go dancing. Studio 54."

"You can get in? I thought only celebrities were let through."

"Honey, I'm Marilyn Fucking Monroe. And don't you forget it."

7

OPENING IN 1977, STUDIO 54 WAS THE HOT-TICKET kind of place a guy like me could only wish of passing through its blacked-out doors.

When Marilyn and I arrived, a wall of people elbowed each other out front in an attempt to be noticed. The bouncer let in a woman I didn't recognize but Marilyn told me was Diana Vreeland, a fashion editor. Like I gave a shit about that. Pigs tried to keep the crowd in line while Steve Rubell stood at the door, his comb-over pronounced, selecting those worthy to enter his Eden. Marilyn had taken some time to do her makeup, blending the mask into her face. She dressed not like Marilyn Monroe, but with dark green hip-hugging bell bottoms, a cropped shirt that let her belly button breathe, and a fur over her shoulders.

Throwing her hand in the air, she caught the eye of Steve Rubell, ready to bring his fantasy to life. When he selected her, I could sense the jealousy from those surrounding. She slipped her fingers in mine and pulled me with force toward the entrance, kissing Steve on both cheeks and then twirling around.

"Divine," he said, ushering us inside.

We passed the coat check where Marilyn left her stole. In the main room, laser lights flashed and an orgy of club-goers danced like tonight was their last on Earth. The sweat, the glitter, even the Disco I normally hated—everything shone bright. A room of smiles, high on drugs and life. Two nearly nude performers on the stage covered only by fig leaves led a pony around in a circle.

"You're a regular here?" I yelled over the music, "Serpentine Fire" by Earth, Wind & Fire.

She tapped her fake nose like Gable had done. From out of her brassiere came a silver thimble. She stuck it up one nostril, inhaled, and then shifted to the other. Her body tingling. She passed it to me and I did the same. Now, I'd done cocaine before, I ain't no saint, but not cocaine that seemed like it was exported straight from Colombia. The kind I knew usually cut with baking soda. A rocket in my nose exploding my brain. I flung my limbs around, pressed Marilyn close, her sweat smelling of cotton candy. Cheek to fake cheek we moved in sync. We kissed and I tasted the coke she'd rubbed into her gums, the world an eternal slide. In this alternate reality we stepped into, I wasn't living back at home with a sick brother and no funds. I shat money. I held power. I had the most beautiful girl in the room on my arm.

The song shifted to a slower tempo, and I wasn't aware that hours had passed except for the strain in my calf muscles. We held onto each other for support. I could swear I heard her crying, but the mask caught her tears. I cried too because I'd never been so happy.

"Let's get out of here," she said, leading me to the exit just like she led me inside. She got her fur from the coat check and we blinked hard at the pre-morning light once we made it onto the street.

"Where do you live?" she asked, slurring.

"Hell's Kitchen but with my folks."

"My place then."

She hailed a cab and we sped downtown stopping at Delancey Street. Walked up four flights to a studio apartment with a bathtub in the kitchen. A sofa, television, exposed piping, and a hollow echo from the high ceiling, a gold shag carpet and a mattress in the corner with an Indian bedspread next to a record player and speakers. A wine bottle with a candle in it and melted crayons dripped down the sides. She flopped on the bed and played Bob Seger, my kind of music. "Still the Same" pumping quietly through the room. She patted the bed and I flopped down too.

She went right for my zipper, forcing down my pants before I even took off my shoes. After finagling off all my clothes, I played with myself a little while I waited for her strip down. She shimmied out of her bell bottoms, flung her crop-top onto a lamp along with her bra, left her panties in a bunch. I went to remove her mask, but she slapped me across the face.

"Hey," I said, my cheek throbbing.

"Don't ever do that." She was serious as hell. Even though I couldn't read her expressions, she was pissed.

"I just want to see you."

"You are seeing me."

She lay back and pulled me on top, forcing me

inside of her. She bucked with dramatic effect, moaning along with Bob Seger.

Afterwards she washed up by the sink while I fiddled around with the record player, moving the needle to "We've Got Tonight". I thought of Cheryl briefly because she always found the song sad. I heard it as uplifting. But Cheryl was a downer so she found most things sad. Marilyn had her back to me, and then all of a sudden, she plucked off her mask and laid it down on the kitchen counter. It seemed lifeless staring back, full of holes. She tapped her nails against the sink and then swiveled around. Her face, nothing like Marilyn Monroe upon first glance. A wider nose, gaunter cheeks, eyebrows with more of an arch. But it was her mouth that vastly differed. Two identical scars extended from her lips practically to her earlobes.

"There," she said, lifeless. "Make you happy?"

I didn't know how to answer.

She put her face in her hands. I was afraid she'd never raise it up for me again.

"C'mere," I said, taking her arm and leading her back to the bed. I had to peel back her fingers.

"You're gorgeous," I said.

"You don't have to lie."

"You are. Marilyn's got nothing on you."

She smiled, causing the scars to become more pronounced.

"Let me tell you what happened, Jake, because you'll imagine a million different scenarios otherwise."

She talked about when she first moved to the city. She didn't say where she came from, this story wasn't about her origins. She was living in a walk-up by 42nd Street before she met Gable. Working as a waitress, she came home late one night and was assaulted on her block. She'd made good tips that night and didn't want to give them or her purse up. She just bought a new clutch she'd been saving up for and she pleaded with the mugger to let her keep it. He had a switchblade, something she never thought he would use. He tugged at the clutch, she tugged back, and then he lost his cool and sliced from her lips to her ear on both sides. She never saw his face since he wore a ladies stocking over his head. And he never really spoke either. He left her there until a hooker found her about a half hour later and got her to a hospital. They stitched her up but the scars would never truly heal.

"I'm sorry," I said. "I would kill the guy if I could."

"He didn't have to cut me like that. He could've pushed me down, taken my money."

"He was a psychopath."

"Everyone's a psychopath. Anyway, I tried makeup to cover the scars but it didn't really work. I kept wait-ressing because I needed the cash otherwise I'd have to move. One day, I was waiting on this guy. He wore a business suit, so put together. The thickest black hair I'd ever seen. Like a movie star. He wasn't Gable then, or at least not in public. He was starting up a business and thought I'd be the perfect fit for his organization. When he gave me my mask—I have to tell you—I'd hid all my mirrors before, I couldn't stand the sight myself. I started cutting, really lashing out, drugs, and not party drugs, *drugs*. I'd do my shift and then go get obliterated. But he gave me a purpose, you see? A brand-new iden-tity. Marilyn Monroe, loved by so, so many. It was really an honor. That he saw I had it in me to be so much more. And now, I'll go outside without Marilyn at times, but the fact that I can always become her, it's like I'm never alone."

I ran my finger from her shoulder to her leg, her skin smooth like milk.

"I get it."

"I so want you to be Errol Flynn too. What the two of us will be able to accomplish—"

"I was sold when I first met you."

We kissed and she spooned against my body.

"There's a job," she said, her voice like a robot now.

"Oh yeah?"

"Not a delivery like before. Not just for a trainee."

"What's it entail?"

"I'm gonna let Gable explain, but I think you're ready. We can do it together."

"I'm glad you showed me yourself," I said.

"No," she said. "I showed you who I used to be. I'm reborn now."

"Yes. Reborn."

She unraveled from my arms, the morning light outlining every curve.

"And you can be reborn too."

8

WITH NARY A WINK OF SLEEP, MARILYN AND I made our way over to the Desire Card's office.

In the pre-dawn, it was hard to find a cab but once we did we sailed through the streets like New York City existed only for us. I still smelled her on me, that cotton candy odor. She wore the mask but tied a scarf around her head along with sunglasses. If someone just glanced, they wouldn't know she had a mask on at all.

At their office, it was the same show as before. Bette hammering away at the typewriter, enough cigarette butts in an ashtray to wonder if she'd been typing all night. She eyed two empty chairs, telling us to take a seat.

Gable's door opened and a masked man stepped out. Gregory Peck. *To Kill a Mockingbird* was one of my folks' favorites. Emile's too. The guy even wore the same kind of glasses and a tweed jacket like he was Atticus Finch in the flesh.

"Marilyn," he said, nodding as he passed. She responded by crossing her legs.

"Old beau?" I asked, once Gregory Peck had left.

"Stay away from him," she whispered into my ear. Bette glanced over and I wondered if she heard.

"Gable, I have Marilyn," Bette said, into the intercom. It buzzed back and we went inside.

Gable was already fixing his early morning martini. I figured a hair of the dog route would be best so I agreed to one and he made it perfectly. Crisp with a twist of lemon. Marilyn declined.

"Thank you for the wheelchair," I said, but he waved me away like it was nothing.

"You did good work," Gable said. "In fact, the client requested you again."

I wondered if she'd told Gable all that happened. I tried to read his mask but it was impossible.

"Marilyn suggested you for a job." He slurped his martini like it was hot soup. "We have a client who believes his girl has been cheating on him. I simply want you both to follow her and report back."

"This is a very important client," Marilyn said. "So I can use the help."

Gable plucked a photograph from his inner coat pocket and passed it over. A pretty woman, mid-twenties with brown hair in a shag cut.

"Wendy McSough. She lives in Alphabet City and works at the women's department at Mays in Union Square. Follow her after work, see where she goes."

He went to his desk and handed me a camera.

"To take pictures of her with another guy."

My heart raced as I looked through the viewfinder.

"You'll check in when you've got something."

We went to leave, but Gable touched my arm.

"Hold on a sec." He turned to Marilyn. "Give us a moment."

"Of course," she said, and left the room.

"Something wrong?" I asked, returning to puberty as my voice skyrocketed to a high register.

"You saw what was in the box you delivered?"

I figured it would be worse to deny so I nodded.

"And she bragged about them, I'm sure. Blood diamonds. How does that make you feel? Ethically, I mean."

"Not one way or the other."

"People died to get those diamonds."

"Yeah, it's not my business."

He swirled around the last bit of martini before gulping it down. His eyes like ink blots seeming as if they were boring into my soul. It was the first time I thought of the devil in relation to him. A quick flash of horns. I felt stupid for it popping into my mind then and grinned. I would only remember it later on when he truly revealed his dark nature.

"In this business, Jake, we are required to look away."

"Yeah, I'm getting that impression."

"Is there anything that might cross the line for you?"

Before I could answer, he continued.

"Of course, the more difficult the wish, the higher pay grade for you. Your brother..."

"Emile?"

"Yes, Emile. He needs surgery."

I couldn't remember if I had mentioned that before. I'd definitely said he was sick so Gable likely figured.

"Yeah, I mean, once they find out exactly what's wrong. Multiple surgeries."

"I can make that happen. I know doctors too. If he needed it, I could make that happen right away." He snapped his fingers loudly.

"That's very kind of you."

"It isn't about kindness. It's about business. If you do for me, I do for you."

I finished my drink.

"But let's see how you do with this job first." He patted me on the cheek, mob-boss style. "Now go, get some rest and report back to me on Wendy's wandering ways."

After I left, Marilyn didn't ask what Gable spoke to me about. We were both tired and went back to her place where we set the alarm and woke up at four in the afternoon to head down to Mays.

Union Square was the pits, a derelict neighborhood with junkies stuffed in the nearby park. Mays dominated the south side. We smoked cigarettes, sandwiched on a bench between two bums, watching the entrance. Around five, Wendy McSough tittered out, her purse held tightly in her fingers, waiting for the crosstown bus. We crossed the street and stood at a far enough distance so she wouldn't get suspicious. The bus finally arrived, coughing down the street, and the three of us got on along with an older woman. Packed at rush hour, Wendy stayed on for three stops until she pulled the cord and we got out with her.

Alphabet City even seedier than Union Square. We followed her down a block with crumbling buildings. She seemed like the head-in-the-clouds type, unaware she was being tracked. At the end of 12th

Street and Avenue B, a man was leaning against the gate of a brownstone. He wore a fedora and whipped it off of his head when she got closer. I got out the camera and snapped a few pictures of them kissing like high school kids, tongues and all. She took his hand and they went inside. On the second floor, a light turned on. The block was quiet and I could hear laughing coming from the apartment. Fleetwood Mac's "Songbird" filled the mournful block. She appeared at the window in a bra before the man embraced her from behind. I snapped a quick picture just in time for her to shut the curtains.

"Good work," Marilyn said. The tickles of the piano coming from Wendy's window caused Marilyn to sway. In her high heels, she danced like the air was her partner. She beckoned me to join and I held her close, rocking to the beat.

"What do we do now?" I asked.

"We dance," she said, to the sinking sun. "We dance until either one of them reemerges." She hummed along with the song. "And I love you, I love you, I love you like never before."

She sang it to me like a threat, like if I didn't love her back, she'd explode. But I did. Even in that short amount of time. I'd been with Cheryl for a year and it wasn't even close to what Marilyn did to me.

"I suppose you want to know about Peck," she said.

I only wanted to keep dancing.

"We dated. Gable frowns upon us mingling, but it's honestly worse if we stray outside of the Card. Anyway, Bette always had eyes on him so that's why she hates me. He's one of those guys who at first seems like a dream and then you peel back the layers and he's rotten inside. Weird fetishes, like extreme. I shudder to think of what I did with him."

"You don't have to get into it."

"You're so tender, Jake, nothing like I'm used to."

The music stopped and the light in the window cut out.

"Wham bam," Marilyn said. We heard feet on the stairs and the front door opened with the man in the fedora bumbling outside. Marilyn unraveled the scarf around her head and shoved it into my hands. "Put this around your head like a bandit."

I did what she said while she ran behind the man in the fedora and stuck something into his back. He threw his hands in the air.

"Take him around the corner," she ordered, her voice different than before. Less Marilyn, more menacing.

I got his collar in my fist and we dragged him to Avenue C. No one on the block except for a bum rooting through a garbage can. The fedora man blubbered for us to take his wallet and leave him alone.

"We don't want your money," Marilyn yelled, spit flying from her lips.

"Please," he said. "Don't shoot me."

I looked down and sure enough a pearl-colored ladies' pistol was clasped in Marilyn's fingers.

"What's your relationship to Wendy McSough?" she asked.

"We're...dating."

"No, you're not. She's with someone else. Did you know that?"

"No, yes."

"Make up your mind."

"She'd been seeing this married guy, but I thought it was over."

Marilyn swatted him across the face with the gun causing blood to spew from his mouth.

"You are never to see her again. Understand."

"I...yes, just please."

She backed up and then drove her high heel into his face, stamping over and over until it became covered with a mask of blood. She laughed through it all, an evil cackle.

"Take a picture," she said to me.

I fumbled with the camera, but managed to snap a photo.

"Remember," she said, her tongue by his wounded ear. "This was the last time you're ever to see Wendy."

"Uhh..." the man said, rolling over on his stomach.

"C'mon," she told me, dashing away. I caught up with her, and she shoved her tongue down my throat flecking my uvula, and then pulled away and gave a twirl, skipping down the rest of the block where she hailed a cab and left the backdoor wide open with her legs dangling out for me to join again, like I'd find myself doing over and over, powerless to resist.

9

GABLE HAD A DARK ROOM ATTACHED TO HIS OFFICE
to develop the pictures while we waited outside.

With Bette typing away, the sound of her hitting
the keys morphed into Marilyn pummeling the face of
the man in the fedora. At first, I was shocked, then a
little scared, but afterwards, horny. No girl I'd ever been
with had a fire in her belly like Marilyn. I found myself
in the back of the cab on the way over to Desire Card
parting her legs and exploring in between. The cabbie
kept eyeing the rearview, and Marilyn played it cool.
Her lips parted, teeth chattering as if it she had a chill.
No indication I was getting her off.

"Must've been nice to see Peck," Bette said, twisting
her mouth into a sour frown. Marilyn was pacing back
and forth and clearly annoying Bette. "Been awhile,
hasn't it?"

"You're free to date him if you want," Marilyn said.

Bette chewed on her cigarette, the smoke obscuring
her face.

"Bitch, I already am."

A smile emerged on Bette's face, the first ever. Marilyn leaned over the desk, parting the smoke curtains.

"Don't call me after he chokes you out while making love."

Bette tilted her neck, revealing a wine-colored bruise. "A present from this morning."

Marilyn balled her hands into fists, her body quaking. Did she still have feelings for that loser? It pissed me off to no end. She excused herself to go to the bathroom as Bette touched her bruises, reliving the fantasy.

I'd always had a tough time dealing with silence. Even though Bette wasn't about to start a convo, I figured I'd find out more about my new girl.

"War between you two?" I asked.

Bette's typing got faster. "I'd define it more as a skirmish."

"She still hung up on Peck?"

Bette ripped out the page of paper and fed a new one into the machine, pushing the carriage back in place.

"She was with child."

"His?"

One shoulder shrugged. "She believed it was his. Then she got an abortion and he lost it."

"Hurt her?"

"He's not what you think. I like it rough. She does as well. She might be all butterflies and rainbows with you now, but that's not her true style. She'll grow bored unless you can keep up."

"Keep up how?"

"You're vanilla, I can tell. And vanilla ain't enough."

"Tell that to the cabbie who just watched us get it on in the backseat."

"Ooooh, you daredevil."

A knock came from outside the office as the front door opened. I expected it to be Marilyn, who wouldn't be happy about me trying to glean info about her from Bette. But a man walked in instead. He was thick and bald, shoulders like mountains, hands like mitts with sausage fingers. He had a permanent expression like you'd just kicked his dog. I'd seen him before, but my brain was working too slow...

"Mr. Mancini, please have a seat," Bette said.

Dick Mancini.

The mobster from Hell's Kitchen who wanted to hire my pop. It'd been awhile since I'd seen Mr. Mancini. In that time, he'd gotten wider and his face had morphed into a beach ball. He sat down next to me, no clue I was Louie's son. We gave each other a polite nod, and he sat back breathing through his mouth. Each exhale a threat.

Bette buzzed the intercom. "Mr. Mancini is here."

"Send them all in," Gable replied.

Dick Mancini barreled into the office while I pointed at myself as if I'd heard correctly.

"Yes, you too," she said. "Go."

I scurried in after Dick Mancini who was already bent over Gable's desk snorting a line of cocaine.

"My new distributor," Gable said to him. "Straight from Colombia. Pure cut."

Dick Mancini pinched his bulbous nose, his blood-shot eyes spinning.

"Like a roller coaster." Dick went in for one more. "Join me," he said, not as an offer but an order. Gable took a tiny toot and waved me over to do the same. The drug a firecracker up my nose, my brain feeling like it was expanding and contracting all at once.

"Jake, meet Dick Mancini."

I was glad Gable didn't say my last name.

"He's our newest trainee," Gable continued.

"I was wondering why he didn't have a mask too," Dick Mancini said, and shook my hand, like being greeted by a beast with a death grip.

"Jake tailed your girl," Gable said. "He took some photos."

He gestured for us to join him in his dark room where a series of photographs were held along a string by clothespins. Various stages of Wendy kissing her guy and then the guy's brutal beating. The last photo looked as if he'd been pelted in the face with tomatoes.

I knew Dick Mancini had a wife and two teenage sons as well. His wife Charlotte liked to get her hair done big so she'd be a commanding presence while she walked down the street. She wore so much makeup she resembled a clown, but a mean clown. I once saw her reaming out a boy who almost hit her with his bike, and I thought she was gonna kill the kid.

Dick chewed on his lips as he observed the photos. He chewed harder when looking at the one of Wendy and the guy kissing. His eyes danced in delight upon seeing the guy beaten.

"I knew it," Dick finally said, ripping off the almost-developed photos from the line and folding them into his coat. "That two-bit whore. She doesn't know how good she had it."

"He's not going see her again," Gable said. "Marilyn made sure of it."

Marilyn appeared in the room. I'd learn she had the power to spring up out of nowhere. A ninja in a white dress.

"She doesn't deserve you, Dick," she said, aping her voice closer to Marilyn Monroe's. For the clients, she didn't want the lines to blur.

"Ah Marilyn, I should just whisk you away to our own private island and call it a life," Dick said, taking her hand and leaving a slobbery kiss. Then he reached into the other side of his coat and pulled out a stack of bills.

"For your troubles," he told Gable, who accepted the cash without counting.

"Would you be able to escort me home?" Dick asked her.

"I need Marilyn for an assignment now," Gable said. "But Jake can take you, can't you Jake?"

"Eh," was all he said. I was clearly not a worthy replacement for Marilyn.

Dick went out of the room and Gable slipped me a few bills.

"For your troubles too," he said, smacking my cheek.

Outside, I hailed a cab, wedging in the back with Dick Mancini, barely any room for myself.

"What's your father think of this?" he asked, once we started moving.

It was stupid to believe he didn't know me. A guy like Dick Mancini knew everything.

"He's not aware."

"Probably best to keep it that way."

He shifted in place so he could reach into his coat pocket for a shorter stack of bills.

"If you keep following her and taking photos, I'll

pay you well," he said, sniffing as if he had a booger stuck in one nostril.

"What about Gable?"

"We cut out the middle man for this," he said, and I wondered if I was being tested. I had no idea what to say. It was awkward leaving him hanging.

"What? Not enough for you?"

"Just...Gable's been real good to me. He bought my kid brother a wheelchair–"

"Listen, you do this or I'll tell your pop what you've been doing." He shoved the money at me. "You're welcome. And if you see that bitch's beau sniffing around her again, feel free to kill him."

He leaned forward in his seat, letting out a putrid fart.

"This is good," he told the cabbie, throwing a few bills into the front seat. "There's a show I want to hit before I head home to the ball and chain. Don't wanna waste that candy cane."

He left the cab and I watched him lumbering down the street before he swung into a strip club on 42nd Street that promised live Dollar Peep Shows. In my hands was more money than I ever made at once, what seemed like almost a thousand dollars. The cabbie was about to drive away but I told him to "wait a minute". I tossed some money into the front seat and made my way out to a strip of XXX clubs, pimps and hookers strolling the block in their furs. I didn't want to waste the candy cane I'd just inhaled either.

I'd been working hard these past few days and deserved some R and R.

10

STROLLING HOME IN THE MIDDLE OF NIGHT singing "When the Levee Breaks" while coming down from a coke and beer high.

Okay, I liked to get obliterated. It was something I was working on. Easier to numb. At home, Pop was eating breakfast, Ma dealing with Emile. Emile was fussing. Mornings the most difficult. I liked to imagine he'd been dreaming he was normal and then woke up all pissed off. Probably Ma too. She dreamed of vacations without playing nurse. I ain't saying she didn't love Emile. She loved him more than me to be honest. But what saint like her didn't deserve a break? Pop probably dreamed about sleeping, since he got so little of it. In the morning, Emile screaming, Pop's eye twitching as he tried to concentrate on a newspaper article about Ghandi being reelected to the Parliament. He usually finished driving the livery cab around two a.m., going back and forth to the airports. All these people traveling all over the world and him shuttle ing between the FDR and I-278.

"Jesus and Mary, you're just getting in?"

"I was celebrating," I said, miming blowing a kazoo.

"Celebrating what?"

I wanted to slam the stack of bills I'd gotten on the table, but it'd look too shady. A thousand bucks? He'd be too suspicious.

"President Carter signed a bill allowing home-brewing beer in the US." I belched to strengthen my point. "Right, Ma?"

I kissed her on the cheek while she tried to feed Emile a scoop of applesauce. Emile had crossed his arms, shaking his head. I respected how stubborn the kid could be. In his small world, if he didn't like something, he'd let you know.

"Hey, Emile," I said. He didn't notice me yet so I took his face in my hands. His features seemed to soften. "Hey, Emile," I said again.

A bunch of words came out of his mouth that sounded like gibberish, but we knew what they meant.

"How's the new job?" Ma asked.

"It's great. I feel like I'm right where I should be."

I headed into my room, flopped on the bed, and didn't wake up until I majorly had to piss and it had already gone dark. I let loose a waterfall in the bathroom we all shared and heard rocks being thrown at my window when I got back. I opened it up as a pebble soared inside. Outside Cheryl looked like Ron Guidry hurling rocks at my head. She had an overstuffed cardboard box with my shit at her feet. I ran out and we got into a screaming match on the street. She wanted my stuff out of her house and to take back anything she left at my place. I told her she'd only been in my room once very early on when we started dating. But she was on her pills and ready to rant at whatever I'd say. I had to take her upstairs, which set Emile off since we didn't have guests over around that time because he ate dinner. My ma was being nice but you could tell it pissed her off. In my room, Cheryl started picking things up and moving them around.

"It's a pair of earrings," she said.

"They're not here."

"Help me look, please."

She wiped her nose a lot and got on her knees searching under chairs.

"They looked like pearls but they weren't pearls."

"I haven't seen anything like—"

"If I don't find them, just gimme the Tiffany's bracelet instead."

"Wait, did you come over here to get the bracelet?"

"No, I'm saying it's only fair—"

"Ya-know, if it means you're out of my life for good..." I rummaged through a drawer and thrust the bracelet at her. Eyes sparkling, she rubbed her hands together. It impressed me the lengths she went.

"Will you help me hail a cab? This neighborhood—"

I ran ahead of her downstairs. As I was about to throw my hand in the air, Marilyn appeared smoking a cigarette on a stoop. She got up, ashed the cigarette, and sashayed over. As Cheryl was coming outside, Marilyn took me in her arms and planted a kiss on my lips like it'd been planned to cause Cheryl dismay. Cheryl still needed a cab so she had to watch Marilyn and I making out. We finally stopped and Marilyn held my hand.

"Hi, I'm Marilyn," she said to Cheryl, holding out her other hand.

Cheryl tried to understand who stood before her. I

wondered if for a second she thought it was the real Marilyn, like I had the first time.

"Cheryl."

"We're lovers," Marilyn said. "It's all very exciting. Jake is very exciting. He brings out something in me I didn't even know existed. Don't you?"

She turned to me as I nodded.

"And I bring out that same wonder in him. He's shining, can you see it? Like he was never shining with you."

Cheryl's face did a dramatic turn. "Excuse me?"

"You're neglectful and sad, a sad woman. You took him for granted. You thought he was a bum. He's a phoenix, baby, and you're an alley cat that hasn't been spayed."

I burst out laughing.

"You're insane," Cheryl said, stifling her own laughter but it was clear she was frightened too. "You two can have each other."

Cheryl began to stomp away but Marilyn grabbed her by the ponytail, yanking her back.

"You dumb trick," Marilyn said, nearly pulling the girl to the ground. Cheryl got her bearings and swung her pocketbook hitting Marilyn in the side. Marilyn scrunched her face and punched Cheryl in the nose. Blood gushed and Cheryl began crying.

"Gable has another job for you," Marilyn said into my ear. The dins of Cheryl carrying on became muted. "He has a car."

She pointed to a Stutz Blackhawk with the word DESIRE on the plate. Gold-plated trim and shag-carpeting on the inside. Spencer Tracy at the wheel. We got in and Spencer Tracy told us a story of when he was a boy back in Finland. He moved to the US with his family when he was a child, but his first memory was driving in a car with them and the black ice on the road caused it to swerve. He thought he was going to die but miraculously the car spun without hitting anything before it came to a slow stop. Everything afterward just borrowed time.

"So, she seemed *nice*," Marilyn said.

"Look, we both have exes we're ready to forget about. Right?"

She was applying lipstick and looking in a compact. She snapped it shut.

"Right."

Back at the Desire Card, Gable had all of us come into his office, Bette and Spencer Tracy included. Gregory Peck too.

"In this business, there are bound to be rivals," Gable said. He sat behind his desk, hands folded as if he was Jimmy Carter giving the Presidential Address. "All this means is we have arrived. There are smaller organizations who wish to be us. They know our turf and are attempting a hostile takeover. For example, the stolen goods enterprise run by Peck. That has fulfilled a lot of wishes, am I correct? It was my idea. Laurence Olivier found it pedestrian, which is why he's better suited running the international office. We each have our strengths. Anyway, there's a tiny organization, a four-man operation at most, but they seem to want the Fish Market, knowing full well the Fish Market is the Card's territory, has been since 1975. I've spent a lot of time getting to know the fishermen. We scratch each other's backs. And now, a threat has appeared. I propose we scare this threat."

There were muffles of agreement from his employees. Marilyn stamped her foot. Gregory Peck punched his fist into his palm. Bette sucked her cigarette even angrier than before.

"We have an ID on these punks?" Spencer Tracy asked, the streetlights creating a diagonal shadow across his face.

Gable removed a photograph and laid it on the desk.

"This is the leader," Gable said, a smirk and a frown fighting for dominance.

I peered closer, my stomach dropping, nearly taking a crap in my pants.

Georgie, my other so-called boss.

11

It wasn't that I cared about Georgie, I just didn't like my worlds colliding.

Gable spoke of Georgie's four-man operation, which included Maggs but also me. No way Gable was this upset about lifted coats being sold down by the FDR; Georgie must've been after a bigger score. Another photo emerged: Jack with the Nose. My bowels swelled as I waited for Gable to pull out a third photograph of Maggs, or even worse, me. The gang would beat me to a pulp and toss me from the second story window. Thankfully, Gable had no other photos.

"Their base is a second story apartment on Pell Street above a dim sum restaurant," Gable said. "We go and put the fear in them. If they back off, we do as well. If not..."

I gulped, audible enough for everyone to look over at my bobbing Adam's apple.

"Spencer Tracy can drive five of us, the others take a cab."

I raised a quivering hand.

"Oh, Jake, right. You don't have a mask." He went in his closet and tossed me a similar faceless one from before. "So you're not recognized."

"I have to make a call."

The gang already began to move out of his office.

"A call?" He stood over me, looking for tells.

"My brother. You know he's sick. I need to make sure–"

"Use my phone and then hop in a cab," he said. "Marilyn'll go with you. 222 Pell Street, apartment 2F as in Fake."

Gable, a master at games. Was he calling me a fake? Did he know I wasn't calling about my brother? He left with the others as Marilyn hung by the door. I picked up the phone, and she watched me carefully.

"It's private," I said. She didn't budge right away. I was afraid she'd never leave and I'd have to make a fake call to my folks instead of who needed to be notified.

"I'll meet you downstairs," she said.

I expelled a sour breath, relieved. She vanished from the door and my shaking fingers dialed.

"Yello?"

"Maggs?"

"Jake, is that you?"

I lowered my voice. "Listen to me. Georgie's operation, right? He's under siege."

"What?"

"A rival gang isn't pleased."

"Jake, you're not making no sense."

"Look, Maggs, we've known each other twenty years. A long fucking time. I've been working for these other guys–"

"What guys? Who are you talking about?"

"It ain't important, just that Georgie's been nudging on their turf. They're headed over to Pell Street now."

"Pell Street, how do you know the headquarters?"

"Maggs, shut the fuck up. Don't go down there."

"Why?"

"Why? They're about to put the fear into them."

"I need to let Georgie know."

"No! I mean, it doesn't matter. If they don't get him now, they'll get him somehow. They only want to scare him. Let 'em scare him and Georgie can find a new turf to sell the coats."

"This is about coats?"

"I don't know. I don't think so. Promise me, Maggs."

"Okay, okay, I'm halfway into a bottle of bourbon anyway."

"Good, go to sleep. Wake up in the morning and tell everyone you were drunk and passed out."

"Ya gotta clue me in on more at some point."

"Okay, okay I need to go, Maggs."

He hung up. I didn't know if it was to get me off the phone, or if he really was gonna go to sleep. Maggs was the type to run into a blazing fire.

When I got downstairs, Marilyn was already in a cab, her legs dangling onto the sidewalk with her signature pose. I shuffled in beside her.

"Brother okay?"

Through the mask, I tried to decipher her eyes. See if they were dubious or concerned. We drove in silence to Pell Street, a wafting smell of fish assaulting our senses upon exiting the cab. Gable and the crew were congregating under an awning since it started to rain. We ran over to them and Gable and Gregory Peck cocked their pistols before placing them in their inner coat pockets. I put on the faceless mask and Gable handed me a gun.

I'd never fired a gun before, not even held one. It was heavier than I imagined.

"You point and shoot," Gable said, because he could tell I was green. I must've looked green too, since a bubble of puke hung in my throat. "Only if you need to."

At the entrance, Gable buzzed all the apartments until someone unlocked the front door. The crew went inside, clomping up the stairs. At 2F, we could hear murmurs coming from the crack. Gable rapped twice. The murmurs got quiet. Gable eyed Peck, telling him to shoot the lock if need be. But the door opened an inch with the chain secured.

Georgie poked his eye through the crack.

"Yes?" he said, trying to display an attitude of authority when it was obvious he was petrified.

"Georgie?" Gable asked, wedging his foot into the crack. "You're going to let us in."

"Who the fuck are—?"

Before Georgie could finish, Gable bashed into the door, snapping the chain and slamming Georgie's head. Georgie doubled back, tripping over his feet. Jack with the Nose was over at a table by the windows playing solitaire. He reached for his piece but Spencer Tracy put him in a headlock first. He wrenched Jack with the Nose to the ground as Bette coolly plucked the man's gun. She kept it trained on Jack with the Nose. Georgie scurried backwards, whipping out his own gun. He took a shot that went nowhere since Peck had kicked his arm, forcing the bullet into the ceiling.

"Where's the rest of your operation?" Gable asked.

Peck had pinned down Georgie, his face mashed under Peck's boot.

"It's just us."

"Bullshit, we heard you had two others."

"They're hired on the side. Who are you?"

His eyes widened as he took in Gable. The slicked-back hair, the tiny mustache. Peck eased up and brought Georgie to a sitting position with a gun jammed in his cheek. I wanted to yell at Georgie to confess about the coats and promise to never sell down by the Fish Market again, but I stayed quiet. Speaking out would only mean I'd receive the same punishment.

"Who we are is not of importance," Gable said. He paced around the small studio apartment, inspecting dirty dishes and opening spider-webbed cabinets. "It's more about how our hairs have crossed."

"We're small potatoes," Georgie said. He was blubbering, on the verge of tears. A man beaten so easily. At that moment, I swore to always remain strong, even when death was sure to follow. "We nab coats outside of Gimbels, Macys, Alexanders. Then we sell 'em hot. That's all."

"No drugs?"

"Well, who isn't in the drug business these days?"

"The coke you unload," Gable said, opening the refrigerator and checking that it wasn't even cold. The freezer hollowed out and stuffed with bags of white powder.

"Who's your distributor?"

"I don't know them, I swear. We've never met face-to-face. The money is left in a secure location and then we come back for the snow."

This was news to me. I had no idea Georgie was in

on the drug game, although I shouldn't have been surprised.

"I have an idea about who your distributor is…"

"Enlighten me. And I'll cut ties. I swear. If you want me to get from you instead…"

"We don't need your business. It isn't about that. You appeared on our radar because you muscled into the Fish Market."

"Consider that over, I promise."

"Let's say our distributor is out of the country. Rather high profile. He's aiming to dominate the market in New York City, already has Miami. Meaning if there's competition, we need to get rid of that competition."

"Please, please," Georgie said, holding his hands over his face, a stream of snot swinging from his nostrils to his lips. "I told you, we're small—"

Gable nodded to Peck, who bashed the gun into Georgie's skull. A dot of blood appeared on the center of his forehead.

"I don't give a flying fuck about you, Georgie, it's all about your distributor. You need to find out who they are so we can ice them."

It was the first I'd heard Gable use that term—*ice*, meaning sure death. I'd see him come through with his promise many times.

"Okay, okay, we could spy I guess," Georgie said. "Wait and see who the bag man is, have him lead you to his boss."

Gable slapped him lightly on the cheek. "Now you're thinking."

Georgie let out an exhale.

"You have your guy set it up, but we're taking you as collateral."

"No, no," Georgie whined, but Gable signaled again and Peck whacked his skull until Georgie finally passed out.

"You," Gable said, to Jack with the Nose. "Set up the exchange and I'll have one of my guys tail you. Then you'll get your boss back."

Spencer Tracy picked up Georgie like a ragdoll and threw him over his shoulder.

"So you can reach us," Gable said, handing Jack with the Nose the Desire Card. Jack read the promise, *Any wish fulfilled for the right price.*

I bet he was wishing he'd pay anything for us all to go away.

12

I NEEDED A SOLID NIGHT OF SLEEP, WHICH WAS
thwarted by a pounding on the front door.

Emile woke up howling, causing my ma to run out
in her nightgown. Pop followed with a wrench in his
fist. There was nothing to be alarmed about because it
was only Maggs, doped up and spooked. Neither of my
folks said hi to him, even though he tried to be polite by
asking how they were doing and apologizing for waking
us up.

"Take it to Jake's room," Pop said, still holding the
wrench like he wanted to bash Maggs's face. We passed
by Emile's room where Ma was feeding him a bottle of
milk, swaddled like an overgrown baby.

Maggs slammed the door and paced from end to
end, tearing out loose ends of his hair.

"I went over to Pell Street."

"Shit, Maggs, I told you not to go."

"I couldn't sleep. Well, I did a couple of lines and
that didn't help. Anyway, the door was busted down
and no one was there."

"They're monitoring Georgie."

"Monitoring him for what?"

"His operation isn't what you think. There's drugs involved."

"Where do you think I get my drugs from?"

"Maggs, these others guys I've been working for are under someone really big. I imagine dangerous too. My boss wants to know your supplier."

"Who's this new boss you got?"

"He owns a company that provides wishes."

Maggs scrunched up his face. "What the fuck do you mean?"

"Like if someone wants something, they can make it happen. Whatever it is. Their drug supplier wants all other rivals out of the picture. You've never seen who makes the drop off?"

Maggs picked up a dart from my desk and rolled it around in his palm.

"Our distributor is a big shot too," Maggs said, throwing the dart at a bullseye board but hitting far from the center. "They all are. That's how they're able to have so many underlings selling for them."

"And you got no idea who?"

"None. Georgie, he might."

"My boss'll beat it out of him if he does."

Maggs sat on the edge of my bed and lay back, his hands covering his face. For a second I thought he was crying, but he was laughing.

"So what do we do now?" he asked.

"*We* stay as far away from Georgie as possible. He's nuclear."

"That may work for you," Maggs said. "But I still need a job."

A knock at my bedroom door revealed my pop holding the phone receiver, the cord tangling all the way back to the kitchen.

"Uh... Marilyn wants to talk to you."

"Thanks, Pop."

"I gotta head to work."

He'd already dressed in his garbage man's garb and slowly handed over the phone as if he knew the insidiousness that existed on the other end. The lies I'd been telling him not only about the Desire Card but Dick Mancini's involvement in their operation too. He'd be crushed if he knew. We'd never been close but I felt an overwhelming sense of love for him. He wouldn't always be around, and I'd miss his gruff presence when he'd be gone. Somehow, I always knew that he wasn't long for this world.

Pop walked away down the hallway, his slight limp dragging his right foot, occasionally using the wall for support.

"Hey, Marilyn," I said, into the receiver.

"There's going to be a drop off tonight at ten p.m. on 12th Avenue and 44th Street right outside the Intrepid once it closes. You need to eye the consigliore."

"The who?"

"The go-between, the distributor's guy," she said. "Jack told us he'd been contacted. We still have Georgie. Jack will be there to pick it up but I need to identify the bag man."

"How?"

"Take pictures. Like you did before. Then stop by our office."

Click.

The busy signal chimed as I rested the phone over my shoulder.

"Was that them?" Maggs asked.

"Yeah, Jack with the Nose is picking up a drop off, I'm there to ID the bag man."

I'd given back Gable's camera, but my folks had a Polaroid.

"Lemme help."

"It's too dangerous, Maggs. Don't get more involved than you already are. Right now, they don't know about you."

"Look, maybe it can help put in a good word with your boss. Like I said, I'm outta work."

"Let's go grab breakfast."

I took Maggs down to the Waverly Diner. He'd never been before. It seemed like a thousand years ago since I'd been there with Marilyn. So much of my life had changed. We got omelets that arrived in a sizzling pan at our table. This time I was able to eat mine without Marilyn rushing me away.

Maggs started telling this story about when we were kids. It was how he got his name. His real one was Edward but he always found it too stuffy. We were like eight and had the wild idea to skip school and drink Robitussin on stoops. We stole a bottle and passed it between us until it was nearly finished. The street started wobbling and I felt like I had to puke but couldn't stop giggling. This homeless man came up to us asking for money. We told him we were kids and didn't have anything. He said he'd fight us for some dough. He hadn't eaten since yesterday and he proved it by showing us ribs poking out of his chest. He said he used to be a boxer. Maggs McMaggsy was his name. He had five TKOs, all men bigger than he. The crowd would chant "Maggs, Maggs," and he never felt so much love. My buddy responded that he was also named Maggs. "That's impossible," Maggs McMaggsy slurred. "I'm the only Maggs." "No, *I'm* the only Maggs," my buddy yelled. Maggs McMaggsy pushed him hard, and my buddy, a little eight-year-old fuck gave him a sharp uppercut that knocked him to the floor. "TKO, you bum," my buddy said. "I'm Maggs now." And he'd been minted ever since.

"The point is, Jake, I've never been afraid of anyone and I'm not about to start now. This new boss of yours, show him I could be a good addition."

"What if Jack with the Nose sees you?" I asked.

"Who cares? I'm not trying to impress Jack with the Nose. C'mon, I got you a job."

"Yeah and look at the hot water it landed me in."

Maggs rolled out of his seat and got down on his knees. "Please, please, please, Jakey."

"All right, all right, get the fuck up, you degenerate." And then I realized how we'd pull it off. "Hey, I have an extra mask."

"What's a mask got to do with it?"

"My boss has all his employees wear masks of old movie stars when they're out in the field."

"And who are you?"

"No one yet, I'm still a trainee. But I have two face-less masks he gave me. You can wear one. That way if Jack with the Nose sees you, he'll just think you're working for the Card."

"The Card?"

"Yeah, the Desire Card. Any wish fulfilled for the right price."

"Sounds shady to me."

"No, man, it's pretty wonderful. I mean, we all have wishes we want to come true, right?"

"I gotta laundry list," Maggs said.

We finished up and headed out into the noon sun. I envisioned working for the Card with Maggs, wondering which movie idol he could be. We'd been together since we were kids and it made sense for us to be at the same organization.

"James Dean maybe?" I said, remembering *Rebel Without a Cause*. I'd been a little kid when I saw it at the theater. This was before Emile. Back then, my folks and I used to do things as a family.

Maggs was stroking his droopy mustache. "What's that?"

"What mask you'd wear. I could see you as James Dean."

"'Dream as if you will live forever. Live as if you will die today'. Didn't he say that?" Maggs asked. "Sure came true for him when his car crashed. Like he knew..."

13

MAGGS AND I DONNED OUR FACELESS MASKS AND hung out around the intrepid waiting for it to close.

A school tour was the last to leave, kids no more than ten years old. Laughing and poking at each other, not a care. I was around that age when my folks had Emile. Before then, Pop only worked as a garbage man and didn't have to drive the livery cab. He was home every night for dinner. We had money for me to play in a Little League and he'd come to my games cheering louder than anyone else's dad. Ma was so young then. Not even twenty-one when she had me practically off the boat from Ireland. She met my father at a Hell's Kitchen pub. She was being hit on by some asshole who got handsy and Pop stepped in. He cracked a pool cue over the guy's skull and Ma melted. They found an all-night diner and talked into the morning. Three months later she got pregnant with me and they married while her belly was still full.

Once the school tour left the Intrepid, the surrounding area stayed pretty empty. Maggs and I found a smart hiding place that gave us good eyes on the drop-off spot. A few minutes later Jack with the Nose showed up. He whistled while rocking on his heels. The Hudson River lapped behind him. Jersey across the way looking like a wasteland. The moon full and painting a shimmering line through the black waters. I blew on my hands holding the Polaroid camera.

A garbage truck pulled up and a man shuffled out from the driver's seat with a bag in his hands. He had a cap pushed low over his eyes. He didn't open the back to throw in any garbage. As I peered closer, I noticed that he also wore a stocking over his face. Jack with the Nose stopped whistling and the two gave each other a firm nod. Jack with the Nose pulled a thick envelope from his pocket and threw it halfway between them. The bag was tossed in the same spot. Jack with the Nose walked to the bag, picked it up, and kept on going, resuming his whistle as he disappeared down the block. The garbage man nabbed the envelope and stuffed it in his uniform. I took a bunch of photos, even though he'd be unrecognizable. But then, my heart fucking sunk into my toes. He limped back toward the garbage truck, leaning against it for support as he hoisted himself into the driver's seat. The same goddamn limp that Pop had.

The garbage truck churned for a few seconds before driving away. I watched the Polaroid dissolve. Although the face was still hidden, the man's build fit Pop's too. It had to be him. All those times he carried on about not working for Dick Mancini when he was in the pocket of some other mobster.

"What is it, Jake?" Maggs asked. "You get a good shot of him?"

Like I'd been punched in the gut, I could barely speak. A wheeze accompanied my crazy admission.

Maggs removed his mask so he could breathe.

I wanted to keep mine on and disappear into its enigma.

As we walked across town to the Desire Card offices, I tried to figure out Pop's motivation. It had to be because of Emile. This was the only way he could get money for Emile's surgeries and therefore I couldn't be angry. I was more afraid. Pop mixed up with whoever ran that operation meant I had to be careful what I told Gable. I was already connected to Georgie and now to Georgie's distributor too. The coincidences kept piling on.

Upstairs, I had Maggs put back on the faceless mask as we waited in the front of the office. I envisioned two scenarios: one where I asked Pop about his involvement, the other where I didn't. If I asked, I'd have to explain how I knew. He couldn't be mad for getting in with the same kind of people he had, but it might make him less upfront about the truth.

"Who's your friend?" Bette asked, while slamming the typewriter keys.

"We grew up together," I said. "He helped me with the stakeout."

Maggs gave a wave.

"New blood," she said. I couldn't tell if she was being cagey or simply making a statement.

"You get a photo of the bag man?" she asked.

"Yeah, but his face was covered."

"What good's that gonna do?"

She finished typing her letter.

"What are you always typing?" I asked.

She gave a look like she was about to cut my throat. Her tongue peeked out of the mask, licking her lips before darting back like a reptile's.

"Reports," she said. "Gable likes to keep a record of everything. In case there's ever a dispute."

"With who?"

"With any of the clients, or the employees. The records become the court."

"What if there's a dispute with you?"

"Oh, I'm impartial."

She read over what she wrote and then filed it into a drawer.

"That from last night?" I asked.

"No, this conversation right now."

The hairs on my arms prickled. Everything we said and did documented. And Bette wouldn't be impartial. She clearly hated Marilyn, and me as well, for associating with her.

I swallowed hard. "Why would Gable be interested in this conversation?"

"He likes to be omniscient, all seeing and knowing. He hates surprises. Like your friend showing up, that's a surprise. How are we to know he can be trusted?"

"I've known him my whole life."

"But we only just met you. We don't even know if you're trustworthy."

We heard a slamming noise coming from the room adjacent to Gable's office.

"The prisoner has awoken," Bette said, observing her nails. She opened a drawer, pulled out a few Mars bars, then opened the door to the room and tossed them inside. We could hear wrappers crinkling and the frenzied sound of chewing.

"Doesn't take long for a man to become a beast," she said. "What's your friends name?"

"I'm Maggs," he said.

She tilted her head as if she was deciding whether or not she approved.

"I wouldn't go in there with Maggs," she said.

"How can I trust your advice?" I asked.

"How could you not?" She reached into her brasserie, pulled out a matchbook. She lit one and chucked it at me. "Or do you like to play with fire?"

"You're full of clichés, aren't you?"

She tapped her fingers against the desk, then pushed the intercom.

"Jake Barnum is here to see you," she said, as the intercom buzzed back. "And he's got a friend with him."

Silence passed from the intercom. The seconds ticked by as my stomach flipped. After about a minute, Gable buzzed back.

"Send 'em in," he said, not sounding pleased.

"Your funeral, baby," she said to me, taking out a nail filer and raking it across her cuticles.

Was Gable upset about my surprise guest? Or had Georgie spilled the truth about our relationship? Did Gable the all-knowing even foresee how my pop was involved?

I took as tiny steps as possible to delay the inevitable, nearly losing the omelet I'd devoured as the door swung open.

14

I was glad to see Marilyn in the office with gable when we entered.

Maybe I was imagining, but she seemed grateful to have me there. Although with the mask, it was always hard to tell.

Gable, at the bar, mixed a row of martinis with lemon twists.

"A visitor," he said to Maggs as he passed him a drink. "Clark Gable here."

"They call me Maggs."

"You helped Jake tonight?"

Maggs gave a nod and sipped the martini.

"I thought it'd be good to have four eyes on the bag man, so we'd get a perfect shot for the photo," I said.

Gable slurped his drink, then placed it on his desk next to a globe.

"And did you?"

I was nervous handing over the Polaroid of my pop. Even though Pop wasn't identifiable, this would set in motion Gable's desire to ID him. There'd be no going back.

Gable observed the Polaroid, holding it to the light in an attempt to see through Pop's head stocking.

"I'm not surprised the bag man showed up with a mask. He's smart like us, I presume."

We all waited for a moment before Gable began cackling and then we joined in, Marilyn's the loudest of all.

"The next time, we take the bag man," Gable said, not laughing anymore. "And force the truth out of him. Are you boys capable of doing that?"

He got close to our faces, breathing hard through his nostrils.

"Of course," I said, and Maggs agreed.

Gable swung back over to his martini and downed the rest.

"So Maggs, you're looking for work?"

"Yeah, Jake said your company grants people wishes?"

"We do. Jake's first assignment was delivering a rare diamond to a woman on Park Avenue. Or sometimes a desire includes having a man ID'd, like our garbage man. Are those jobs you would be apt to do?"

"Yes," Maggs said. "Very much so. My last employer..."

I kicked Maggs's foot.

"Let's just say, I'm fully available now," Maggs said.

"Well, for the time being, you have a mask," Gable said, nodding to the faceless mask in Maggs's hands. "You can follow Jake on assignments and we'll see about hiring you full time."

"Thank you, sir. Thank you so much."

"The pleasure is all mine," Gable said, but it didn't sound like it was. I might have been reading too much into Gable's body language, but it seemed like a show he was putting on for Maggs. Once my friend would leave, I'd experience his true wrath.

"If you'll wait outside," Gable said, showing Maggs the door, as if on cue.

Maggs shot me a look given to someone about to be executed. He placed his hand on my shoulder and left.

"You're sweating, Jake," Gable said. I could smell it, the rankness from my armpits.

"It's hot in here," I said, glancing over for Marilyn to agree.

"Are you hot, Marilyn?" Gable asked, and she shook her head.

"No, the temperature is quite pleasant in here."

"Sir." I took a deep breath, wondering if it would be my last. "I apologize for bringing my friend along. I really thought it would help–"

Gable raised his hand, silencing.

"It's quite all right. Are you afraid that I'm upset?"

"Yes, I would never–"

"I welcome recruits to our cause, just as I've welcomed you."

Marilyn began rubbing my back. I was quivering and her touch managed to soothe.

"We want our organization to grow and your friend seems like he could be a good fit," Gable said.

"Oh okay, far out, man."

"But that isn't why I've brought you in here."

"No?"

"No." He held up the Polaroid. "This man is the key."

"I'm sorry we couldn't see his face."

Gable glanced at Marilyn who gave a telling nod back.

"You see, this man's boss, we have an idea of who he might be, but we need conformation."

"For our client," Marilyn added.

"Yes, a very high-profile client. Someone who could bring us much business. But not if the bag man's boss is still in the picture."

"What do you want me to do?"

"Good, Jake, always thinking of the next step. I see greatness in you. First, this boss needs to be revealed, then we will decide what to do with him."

I knew this kind of speak referred to murder. I'd never pretend I was naïve. But how bad could the world be with one less mob boss? I rationalized I was doing society a favor.

"Oftentimes the bag man ain't aware of the higher-ups," I said. "Just like the man you got locked in the room."

"What are you saying?" Gable asked.

"We use the bag man to get us to his boss, but he's not essential."

"Georgie told us the drop-offs happen once a month," Marilyn said. "So we gotta wait a long time before our next move."

"Let me try," I said, gesturing for the Polaroid. "I've seen the guy, the way he walks, Maggs did too. We can investigate the garbage collectors. I'm guessing the drop-off point was on his route."

Gable handed back the Polaroid. I felt my pop was safe once it was back in my hands, as if I could steer all of this in the direction I wanted.

"I like your moxie," Gable said. "Reminds me of myself when I was your age."

"I think it's time," Marilyn said, nudging him.

"I do as well."

Gable went to his closet. He could be pulling out a gun to end me, but I was convinced I had them on my side. I'd never really been part of an organization before. If a bullet was meant for me then, I'd certainly be surprised but not gobsmacked. A mask appeared in his hands instead.

"Here you go, Robin Hood."

The face on the mask had a winking smile, a thin mustache, and wavy black hair. I slipped it on. Certainly good looking, the kind of guy everyone trusted as a friend.

"It's Errol Flynn," Marilyn said. "Congratulations, you were meant to be him all along."

Gable squeezed my shoulder in a fatherly way. With the masks on, we looked as if we could be related.

"Fits perfectly," Gable said, squeezing my shoulder again. Hard enough to feel the burn.

Afterwards, Maggs went home but I was wired so Marilyn and I took a cab to her place. She insisted I wore my mask while we made love. Errol Flynn and Marilyn Monroe together at last. We didn't have time for prophylactics. When I came inside of her, it gave us both the chills. The windows had been left wide open and we shivered on the soaked sheets. I might have told her I was in love, since we brought a bottle of bourbon into bed. I wasn't worrying about Pop. I knew I'd have to later on. The future far enough away, and I deserved a celebration. Damn proud of rising up the ranks of the Card in such a short time. I'd figure out a way around Pop getting into trouble and still shine in Gable's eyes.

We lay back and smoked cigarettes through the masks and Marilyn fiddled with her record player. Jackson Browne's "Running on Empty" came up, but I was far from running on empty: exhilarated, nestled into Marilyn's poof of acrylic blonde hair. She hummed along to the song and so I did as well.

The sun rose and fell and we remained stuck to her bedsheets and each other. She rolled over, heavy against my chest, an anvil pressing into my heart. Hard to breathe, but I wouldn't have traded being crushed by her charms for any other wish on the planet.

My wild witch tracing a finger through my chest hair, pinching a nipple and lapping up a dot of blood, staining her lips ruby red as she continued her spell.

1979

15

1978 CAME TO A CLOSE WITH CHICAGO SERIAL
killer Jon Wayne Gacey arrested and Jim Jones leading
his Peoples Temple cult in a mass-murder suicide that
claimed over nine hundred lives. I was spending New
Years at Theodora Birch's with a medley of her snooty
friends and other members of the Card. She wore the
brooch I'd delivered, boasting to her guests about her
rare blood diamond. They all seemed to salivate. The
Card's employees wearing our masks: Marilyn and
Peck, Bette and Spencer Tracy. Word was the members
of the international office would be arriving—Laurence
Olivier and Katherine Hepburn. I roamed her Park
Avenue apartment, since I hadn't gotten a chance to see
it beyond the living area. Tall ceilings with crown mold-
ing, heavy drapes like she lived in another century,
paintings on the wall that cost more than my pop
earned in a year. She liked nudes: men and women, all
voluptuous in various stages of intercourse. I was
studying a rather full bush as I tried to wrap my mind
around the last two months.

For one, there'd been a lot of Marilyn, her bush full enough to braid, not blonde but a brownish red. We'd fallen into a pattern of sleeping through mornings, having coffee and Irish lunches, then heading out on assignments. Obtaining these fancy cigars imported from Cuba for one client. A necklace made of gold from Jesus's era. These objects tricky to track down, but thrilling once we did. The more dangerous wishes taken care of on my off-time.

Dick Mancini still wanted me to eye his girl Wendy McSough and make sure the guy with the fedora never showed up again. At around five o'clock, I'd tail her from Mays with my Polaroid, but the guy never surfaced. I imagined we scared him good. I'd gotten used to Wendy's habits. Sometimes she stopped for a malted at this shambles of a diner. She sipped with a straw, flipping through a paperback novel. When she got home, she turned on her record player. She liked Fleetwood Mac and sometimes played Carly Simon or Joni Mitchell. Occasionally she sang, always alone, no girlfriends, a sad existence. A few times I heard her crying by the window. The only visitor she ever had was Dick Mancini, who brought gifts in big boxes tied with a bow. I could tell she didn't like him too much. He was twice her age and had a walrus quality to him. Big lips that looked as if they wanted to be hoovering some shrimp cocktail. He was handsy with her on the street. One time I heard them making love. When he came, he sounded like a bus stopping at a station. He winked at me after he left her place. Once a week, I found an envelope with two crisp hundred-dollar bills in the mailbox. I never mentioned it to Gable, but had an eerie feeling that he already knew. He had an uncanny ability to ferret out the truth.

My other job required ID'ing the bag man at the next drop-off. Gable had released Georgie after beating him up pretty good. Georgie got word for the next transaction (still without a clue that I was connected to the Card), but the bag man never showed. Jack with the Nose waited into the night and I had as well. I wondered if it was because Pop had gotten wind. I tried to figure out a way to ask Pop but didn't know how. I asked about his garbage route once and was met with a shrug of his shoulders and hocking of some phlegm stuck in his throat. I asked about driving the livery car, which had to be a front, but he was invested in a news-paper article and made that clear by crinkling the pages in annoyance as he turned them. After watching him down six Schlitzs one early morning, I got up the nerve to find out if he had a third job.

His garbage shift was starting in about an hour and he hadn't been to sleep yet. The rings under his eyes purple like pizza gets when left out in the sun. He looked older than his fifty-two years. Once someone resembled an old man, they'd never return to youth. I remembered him hoisting me on his shoulders as a kid. Now those shoulders had stooped so much, full of knots. His breath oozed beer and his gut fought for room with the dining table, losing out. He closed one eye, twisting his face in way that made it known he wasn't engaging in my questions. He crushed the can, let out a belch, and limped into the bathroom.

That was actually the last time we saw each other since I'd been staying over at Marilyn's most nights and avoiding him the others. Part of me thought if I pretended he wasn't the bag man, then magically it'd come true. I was working for people who got all their wishes granted, why shouldn't I deserve one too?"

"Like what you see?" a throaty voice asked me from behind. In the dim hallway light, I tried to make out who it belonged to. Two toots of coke and three fingers of whiskey made it tough to do anything but sway.

"That was me in my younger days," the voice continued, as I turned away from the nude painting. A light flipped on and revealed Theodora Birch wearing a see-through shawl and a body-clinging ocean-blue dress. I wanted to throw her back in the waters.

"But my pussy is still an abyss," she said, leaning against the wall and stroking the wallpaper. She kicked out a leg and purred.

"I should be getting back to the party," I said, but she blocked me with her arm.

"Want to go cave diving," she said, not as a question.

"Uhh..."

She yanked me into a room and flopped on a fainting sofa. She wedged her dress up and slid her panties down by her ankles.

"This is what I desired," she said, rotating her hips. "Already paid the Card."

"I didn't know—"

"It doesn't matter."

She grabbed my tie and pulled me toward her crotch.

After freshening up in the bathroom later with a liter of mouthwash, I returned to the party where she gave me cat-eye glances from across the room.

"Errol," Gable said, directing me over to the

window where the backs of a man and woman stood. "Sorry about Theodora. Would it help to hear she paid ten thousand for that dalliance? She always wanted to have Errol Flynn eat her out."

"A head's up would've been nice," I said, and an awkward silence sat between us. He didn't laugh. I had to learn that while Gable made jokes, he didn't appreciate them at his expense.

"Olivier," he said, and the man and the woman turned around. She was tall with broad shoulders and a youthful Katherine Hepburn mask. When she held out her hand to shake, it had liver spots galore.

"Katherine," she said, the voice a perfect mimic. It brought me back to watching *The African Queen* with my folks on the tiny black and white TV we first owned. She and Bogart so small I could barely make them out, but I was still mesmerized. Like I was shaking hands with royalty.

"Errol Flynn," I said, not yet used to that being my name.

"Olivier," Laurence Olivier said, with a slight accent I couldn't place.

"Our international arm is rather new," Gable said. "But burgeoning."

"Europeans tend have a desire for even finer things," Olivier said. "I've heard good things about you from Gable."

"Errol moved up from trainee to full timer in record time," Gable said, and I couldn't help but beam.

Classical music was playing from an old phonograph. The record cut off and Theodora Birch clinked on her champagne glass to get everyone's attention. The room quieted. She had a grin on her face so large. She kept licking her lips as she spoke.

"Ten seconds till 1979," she shouted, and all the guests began to count down. At midnight, some sang "Auld Lang Syne" while I searched for Marilyn to kiss. Peck and Bette were tonguing in the corner. Olivier and Katherine Hepburn pecked. I saw Marilyn in Gable's arms and he planted a kiss as a shiver crawled down my spine. The kiss told me this wasn't their first time. When their lips parted, she and I locked eyes and she was spooked. Gable had already moved on to another girl and Marilyn bounced over.

"It's a tradition we have," she said.

"It's fine."

"It doesn't mean anything."

"He's the boss, it's really fine."

"I love you."

We had said it before to one another, but mostly in the throes of passion where it didn't count. She batted her eyes waiting for me to reply.

"I love you too."

She curled into my shoulder and we kissed again, but the masks kept our lips at a distance. I wanted to take both of them off, except I rarely removed my own anymore. It had fused into my skin and felt weird without it on.

We wandered away from the main room because we were starting to take each other's clothes off in front of everyone. With her collarbone between my teeth, I unzipped the back of her dress, left it in a pool on the floor. As we groped toward a bedroom, another couple had already stolen our idea. They sat on a giant bed, faces close, whispering.

"Who is it?" Marilyn asked, giggling in my ear.

A stream of moonlight poked through the drapes and outlined their faces, Olivier and Hepburn. When Marilyn noticed who it was, she put a finger to her lips.

"Makes my blood boil," Hepburn said, in her mid-Atlantic accent.

"I despise him more," Olivier replied.

"What are we going to do about it?"

He ran his fingers through her fine, fake hair. "Wait for the right time to pounce."

Marilyn quietly pulled her dress back up and descended into the dark of the hallway. She motioned for me to come.

"Did you know?" I asked, once we were out of earshot.

"What, that Olivier is a snake? We're all vipers."

"Do we tell Gable?"

"If you want to be the messenger."

"Doesn't the messenger sometimes get shot?"

"Darling, it's all a crapshoot with Gable. Never know if you're rolling snake eyes."

If I'd say anything to Gable, I'd wait until after the party. I wouldn't want to ruin 1979 before it even began.

16

I GAVE GABLE THE APPROPRIATE AMOUNT OF TIME the next morning before I showed up at his office to deliver the news.

I also had a pounding headache from all the drugs and alcohol I'd consumed. When I woke up in Marilyn's bed, she was already gone and left a note saying she was on assignment. We hadn't talked about it the night before, but she was often working on things "above my level of clearance." I swiped a pack of cigs from off her counter and decided to walk to the Card's offices. The city pretty empty, most still sleeping off their hangovers. Garbage piled up along the sidewalks due to the strikes causing a foul odor that usually didn't show up until summer. Derelicts traded needles while young punks tagged a storefront and looked over their shoulders for pigs. It was unseasonably warm and I only needed a cool leather jacket I'd recently bought. The last time I owned one as nice, it had been stolen.

I thought of how to frame what I saw to Gable. He deserved to know, and it could also make him trust me even more. Especially since I'd been close-lipped about a few things that needed to stay hidden for a little longer. And while the messenger sometimes got killed, I was confident Gable would be glad to hear the truth.

Inside the office, Bette was already going to town on her typewriter. Did that woman ever sleep? She gave me a grunt in lieu of a hello.

"The boss in?" I asked, and she blew a stream of stroke from the side of her mouth, which meant yes.

I knocked on the door to find Gable perched at his desk like he was waiting for me. A tumbler of what looked like rye at his side.

"Errol. Enjoyed the party?"

I fixed my mask because I had put it on in haste. I always felt I had to look perfect to him. He seemed to smile bigger once it was more centered.

"Very much so. I'm enjoying this new world."

The words sounded funny out of my mouth, but it was really what I'd been feeling. The rich. The powerful. I'd never had a glimpse of them before. In Hell's Kitchen, we lived in rickety walk-ups with bad plumbing and families of cockroaches. Owned glassware with patterns that were beginning to chip and peel. A Sunday roast that had to be stretched to Tuesday. Half the kids I knew dropped out of school, never got a GED, never thought about college. Most wound up in jail, a few of the truly unlucky shipped to prisons. We didn't have much to celebrate.

"I'd like to be able to show it to you," he said, and shot out his hand to offer me a seat. "That's what we aim for. Fulfilling our clients' desires but also our employees. You are the heart of the Card."

He reached into his wallet and pulled out ten hundred-dollar bills.

"For your services last night."

"I was happy to do it."

"No, you weren't. But it showed your dedication, that's why I offered the desire."

"Oh."

"A hazing of sorts."

I stuffed the bills in my pocket.

"I have something to tell you."

He cut the head off a cigar and placed it in his mouth. "Yes?"

"It involves other members. I've been debating how to say this."

He lit the cigar, puffed rings. "I'm going to explain something, Errol. The Card has many arms, I am its head. I direct the flow. But sometimes, an arm wants to do differently than the brain. This does not make for a fully functioning body."

"Yeah, that's what I thought."

"I've gotten rid of employees before. I strive for a precise fit. So, if you have information..."

"Okay, me and Marilyn..."

I instantly regretted mentioning Marilyn since she wasn't there, but it was too late.

"We wanted to mess around. We've been seeing each other."

"I hope that isn't your big reveal."

"No, I mean... I hope it's cool. I dig her. I dig her a lot."

"She's an enigma wrapped in a riddle stuck in a puzzle and I mean that in the most endearing way."

"Yeah, so we were headed into a bedroom to mess

around and saw Olivier and Katherine Hepburn. They were in the dark, didn't notice us at all. They were discussing you."

He gripped his glass of rye so hard I thought it might shatter.

"Tell me exactly what they were saying."

"Talkin' shit about you. How they were waiting for the right time to pounce."

He puffed his cigar, didn't reveal his displeasure.

"Thank you," was all he said.

"Are you mad?"

"At you? No, Errol. You did right by telling me."

"I didn't want to upset you."

"I would've been more upset if I didn't know."

"What are you gonna do about it?"

"You may go, Errol." He flicked his wrist at the door.

"I didn't mean to pry..."

"You may *go*."

It was as if flames licked under his tongue. I was spooked enough to shoot up in my seat and scurry to the door. I shouldn't have been nosy, but at least he was happy I shared the information. As I left, I caught a glance of him running a finger around the edge of a glass, making it sing, the noise so loud and sharp it stung my ears.

As I walked back home, it had started to flurry. From being so warm before, I was chilled in my leather jacket. I wanted to go home so I could rest, since I knew if I went back to Marilyn's we wouldn't be able to keep our hands off each other. As I neared my folks' block, I noticed a van creeping up with tinted windows, sketchy as hell. I checked my pockets if I had switchblade on me, but left it at Marilyn's. The van stopped and the door swung open. I spun around ready to attack but Georgie jumped out. One of his eyes swollen and closed.

"Get in," he said.

"I...was just headed to my folks'."

"Get. In."

I lowered my head and lumbered inside his rape van. Had he found out I was working for the Card? That couldn't be good. A million excuses ran through my skull, but none seemed like they could explain sufficiently.

The van door shut and Jack with the Nose gunned the gas. My folks' place receding in the rearview. Georgie could think I had something to do with him being beaten and do the same to me.

"We're in trouble," Georgie said, speaking as if he sucked on marbles, his face still swollen too. "Need your help."

I breathed a sigh. If they needed my help, that meant they wouldn't be kicking my ass.

"Turns out we've gotten in with the wrong kind of guys. We've been involved in the coke trade. Maybe not the smartest of our pursuits." Georgie sniffed. A wedge of cotton had been jammed up one nostril. "Stepped on the wrong turf, ya-hear? The boss we've been getting our coke from needs to be ID'd. This is where you come in."

I gulped. "Okay."

"ID'ing ain't working since the guy's bag man wears a stocking over his head. So we need to take the bag man and get him to ID the boss whose turf we stepped on, ya-hear?"

I nearly shit myself.

"This isn't an ask, it's a command. You work for us, Barnum. Maggs too. Anyway, we found out this bag man is gonna make a drop in a week. You, Maggs, and Jack need to nab the guy and throw him in the van. We'll torture him until he reveals his boss." He glanced out of the window. "Park here, Jack."

Jack slowed the van and Georgie opened the door, edged me out.

"We'll be in touch, Barnum."

The van roared off spitting out fumes. The snow falling at enough of a rate to make me shiver. I ran through slushy puddles until I was home and safe, but would I ever really be safe with these gangs of degenerates at war with me in the center?

17

I DIDN'T EXPECT POP TO BE HOME WHEN I GOT upstairs, but there he was hunkered at the dining table with a schlitz in his fist.

"Ma took Emile to a doctor's appointment," he said, and took a sip. He jiggled the can to see what was left, then tossed it in the garbage.

I spun around a chair and sat with my elbows draped over the back. "Everything okay?"

"Kid's been puking all day. Saoirse called the dispatch so I came home. They'd already gone. I'm waiting by the phone." He eyed the rotary hanging in the kitchen. "Hasn't rung yet."

"Hope he's okay."

"Kid's never gonna be okay." Pop rose on cracked knees and limped to the fridge, nabbed a Schlitz then grabbed another. "Here."

We sipped, praying for the phone to cut through the silence. He massaged his leg, winced in pain.

"Acting up on ya?" I asked.

"Product of age. I'm old enough to know it's not gonna get any better, only worse."

"Should you be drinking if you're driving the livery car tonight?"

"Called in sick, in case your ma needed me."

I handed over the envelope with the money I just got.

"This can go for Emile's doctor visits."

Pop squinted as he counted the bills, not trusting their source.

"A thousand bucks?"

"Yeah, from my new job."

"This mystery job..." He let the bills float from his hands.

"It ain't a mystery. Georgie, I've been working for Georgie."

"Yeah, you've said as much. Don't know him."

"Maggs got me—"

"The job, yeah you've said that too."

"Pop, there's something I gotta tell ya."

A car passed by outside blasting Barry Manilow's "Can't Smile Without You," like anyone should be proud of listening to that dreck.

"I think I saw you..." I chewed my lip as I figured out how to continue. "Delivering."

"Delivering?"

"Yeah, about a month ago. I was with Maggs down by the Intrepid. You know the museum with all the fighter jets?"

"I know what the fuck it is."

"This garbage truck pulled up and a guy stepped out with a bag."

I tried to read his eyes, but he was giving me nothing. I caught a glimpse of the garbage can which held about six empties and wondered if I should've waited until he sobered up.

"He had a limp."

Pop's pupils traveled at a glacial pace over to his leg.

"And a stocking over his face."

"Wasn't me."

"Pop, listen to me..."

"No, you listen to me. I don't know what kinds of shady dealings you're involved with. Out at all hours, barely returning home."

"I'm bringing in cash."

"What's this money from? Is it dirty?"

"No, it's honest. Georgie gets me gigs. Driving him around. Getting him things he wants. Deliveries."

Pop pointed at me, his finger tracing circles because of his drunkenness. "Maybe *you* were the delivery guy you think you saw?"

"If you're in any trouble?"

He slammed his chair into the table and stood on one shaky leg. Chewed on the air for bit as he tried to find his words.

"You worry about yourself. You're the one who's been in jail. Not me, bub."

"If you're mixed up with the wrong people."

He went to take a swing at me, but missed in a sad way. Spinning around and fighting with himself. I jumped up and had to hold him steady.

"Get offa me."

"I'm here for you, Pop. That's all."

"Well, I don't need ya."

He pushed me off, shuffling toward his bedroom. The lock on the front door turned and Ma came in with Emile, her cheeks red. Emile rarely left the house so carrying him up the three flights of stairs along with a wheelchair ain't easy. Her red hair had escaped from the rubber band holding it back and cascaded down her shoulders in a fiery swirl.

"Oh, Jake. Jakey, help me here."

She was having a hard time wedging the wheelchair through the doorframe. We backed it out and managed to pull it through. Emile seemed doped up, his eyes off in another world.

"How's Emile? Pop told me."

"Where's your father?"

"Think he went to take a nap."

"Let's not bother him yet."

She pushed Emile into a corner of the living room and turned on the TV so he could watch the $25,000 *Pyramid*, which he enjoyed. Even though he didn't understand what was going on, he clapped when the contestants won and looked happy.

"He stopped throwing up." Ma charged to the fridge, took out a bottle of milk, and chugged it like it was alcohol. "Ah, fuck it." She poured herself a glass of Irish instead, nodded to me if I wanted one as well. I never turned down Irish.

"Do they know why?"

"It's his guts, they're in tatters the doctor says. He's a quack. Gave me a list of all the foods he shan't be eating. There's nothing left. Basically, I can boil potatoes and feed it to him mashed."

"I'm sorry, Ma."

"Ain't you who has to be sorry, Jakey. Ah, I'm at my wits." She fell onto the couch and I joined her. Emile had tilted his head to the side and we sipped and watched the *Pyramid*.

"The money," I said, and leaped up to grab the thousand backs. I placed it in her hands. "For all the doctor's visits. Anything the insurance doesn't cover."

"Ah, Jakey, I can't take this of yours."

"No, Ma, I'm happy to give it to you. It's why I'm doing what I'm doing."

That was a bald-faced lie, but at the time I'd convinced myself it was at least part of the reason. Truth was, while I enjoyed helping the family, being a part of Card was an adrenaline rush like no other.

She kissed my cheek leaving a lipstick stain. "I haven't seen you in a while. Where've you been staying?"

"At my girl...friends'."

It was the first time I'd referred to Marilyn as my girl and it felt great. Ma seemed to soften at the mention of her.

"I figured it was a girl. Tell me about her."

"She's an old soul," I said. "Real pretty too, like... like Marilyn Monroe."

"Oh, divine. She was one of the most beautiful women on the planet. Such a tragic end."

"Yeah, I've always thought so too."

"Remember going to see *Some Like It Hot*? Ah, you were just a kid. We saw it at the Ziegfeld when they brought it back. You had stars in your eyes the whole time."

"No, I remember it well. We went to Carmine's after."

"Did we?"

"Think that was the last time."

"Well," she said, glancing over at Emile and then looked ashamed of herself. "I should check on your father."

"I love you, Ma."

"Oh, Jakey, I love you too."

She squeezed my knee as she got up with her glass and made her way to the bedroom slow as possible like she dreaded the outcome.

"Watch your brother," she called from the hallway.

Emile stayed slack, only blinking and breathing heavily like he usually did. Then his eyes shot my way like they knew the burden he caused on us and they apologized even though there was nothing he could do. I went over and hugged him, wiped the drool from his mouth, and sat beside him watching the *Pyramid* and *Hollywood Squares* and *The Match Game* and the *Newlywed Game* where a contestant answered the question of, What's your husband's greatest happiness? The wife held up a sign that said, Makin' Whoopee. The audience cheered and Emile let out a long howl. Sitting with him for those few hours, I'd forgotten about all the messes I'd gotten myself into. It was just me, my kid brother, and the boob tube.

Wasting away the day like every fucking American family out there.

18

I LEFT AROUND FOUR O'CLOCK TO GO FOLLOW Wendy McSough.

Mancini tasked me to do this now twice a week. If she was still seeing her man with the fedora hat, odds were I'd catch them at one of their rendezvous. She left Mays Department Store like she always did, clutching her purse and riding the bus three stops before getting off. Today she stopped in a diner she sometimes frequented and got a malted. She managed to smile when it arrived, then dove into a book, *The Thorn Birds* by Colleen McCullough. It looked boring but she was invested, flipping the pages and sometimes folding down a corner. When she finished the drink, she left three single bills, but exited the diner without her purse.

I waited a second in case she came back, but then saw her passing by the window unawares. I nabbed the purse and dashed outside, chasing her down the block.

"Oh my," she said, her hand against her forehead. "How silly of me."

"I had to come after you," I said, almost telling it to myself.

"If my brain weren't screwed on..."

We laughed. She had a forced giggle, timed to explode when she was nervous.

"Wendy," she said, extending a hand.

"Uh, Jake."

Was she flirting? This wasn't good. Or maybe it was? Maybe I could find out if she was still seeing her old paramour.

"Can I buy you another malted?" I asked. "I saw you were drinking one. I love 'em too." She was about to say something and closed her mouth.

"I'm kinda full from malteds."

There was that laugh again.

"Oh."

"This is me," she said, flicking her wrist toward her house. "Can I ask you up for a drink? I have some sherry. It's the least I can do."

So we went up to her apartment that I knew in full detail. A poster of "The Endless Summer" on the wall along with Max Ehrmann's "Desiderata," macramé plant hangers and yellow and orange wallpaper. A mirror shaped like a flower and a Big Bird-colored beanbag chair. A crocheted afghan draped over the couch and one of those armed pillows women like to call "husbands."

She hung up her coat, went to her little kitchenette, and poured two glasses of sherry. We clinked.

"What do you do, Jake?"

"Odds and ends. Little of this..."

"Little of that?"

She had a pretty smile that showed off lipstick colored fire engine red.

"Jack of all trades," I said. "*Jake* of all trades," I continued, being flirty.

Her laugh came sharp and quick. She had finished her sherry and poured another.

"I shouldn't," she said, but kept pouring. "Tough day at work. My boss, well he's a creep, touched my ass today."

"I should kill him."

"You," she said, directing her index finger into my chest.

"Or you should have your boyfriend do it."

She frowned and slipped off her high heels, rubbed her feet.

"You'd think," she said. "It's complicated."

"I know how it is."

"Not like I have. Got one fella I can't see and one who tries to see me too much."

"Popular girl."

"I should be married with kids by now. I'm almost thirty. Should have a sweet guy taking care of me, someone to rub my feet after a long day."

"So why can't you see the guy you like?"

"He up and vanished when things were getting real heavy between us. The bum. He's a bum. A salesman. Sells suitcases. Has a store down on the Lower East Side. Nice leather."

She directed her chin toward a leather case in the corner that seemed unused.

"He promised me a trip to Hawaii, where's my lei?"

She found this funny.

"So, you haven't seen him in a while?"

"Long time, but I'm thinking of going down to his store. Just showing up and being like, Craig, hey Craig, remember me? Remember Wendy? We were good together. And then you vanished."

"I'm sure he had his reasons."

She cocked her head to one side. "Uh uh, no, no. No good reasons. Just a vanishing act."

"What about this another guy?"

"He's a big shot." She puffed out her cheeks. "One of those scary types. But he treated me nice. Has connections. You know, con-nect-ions. Wise guy. Stupid of me but he buys me nice gifts. Like this dress. I know I should tell him to shove off, but on my salary, it ain't easy to afford dresses."

"Sure."

She jumped up, the alcohol spilling from her glass as she slammed her feet into her high heels. "That's it! I'm gonna see him."

Sweat pooled on my forehead. "Who?"

"My guy. Craig. My true guy." Her eyes welled up. "Cause I love him. I really do. And I don't care, I wanna hear it from his mouth if he ain't into me." She grabbed her coat. "If I leave now..."

"I think this is a bad idea," I said, moving to take her coat off but she stayed firm.

"It's the best idea I've had, probably ever. I'm gushing right now. I haven't smiled like this since I saw him last."

"What about your other guy? He couldn't be too pleased."

"He don't own me. He thinks he does but he already has a wife. He can boss her around, I'm through with it."

She grabbed her keys and was out of the door before I could say anything. I followed her into the hallway where she locked up and rushed down the stairs. This was becoming a disaster.

"Come with me," she said, once we were outside. "You can make him jealous, yes that's perfect." She threw her hand into the air to hail a cab. One arrived before I could say anything and she yanked me inside. She told the cabbie the address and in minutes we pulled up to a tiny store on Eldridge Street. She left the cab without paying, leaving me with the fare. By the time I paid, she was inside. When I followed her in, she was reaming out her guy who was still wearing his signature fedora. She called him every curse in the book, enough for an elderly customer to shuffle outside plugging her ears. The fedora guy's face had cleared up from the beating he'd gotten. He started crying. He told her how much he loved her, but he was told to stay away from her. "By who?" she asked. "Who do you think?" he yelled. "He had his sadistic crew knock me around." "I hate him, I hate him, I hate him," she wailed, and then the two of them started kissing like I wasn't even there. They were devouring each other and then he picked her up. She wrapped her legs around his body, and they moved to back room tripping over suitcases along the way. Moans could be heard along with her wild laughs. I left the store, worse off than when I decided to return her purse. Once Dick Mancini would find out about their reunion, I might've sealed both their death warrants.

It was dark as I headed back to Marilyn's, no money left for cabs or even a subway token. Having to walk miles through slushy snow in my wet kicks.

19

Arriving at Marilyn's, I smelled a honey scent upon opening the door that let me know she was already there.

Cooking up something over a pot in her kitchen. Mask sweating from the steam. The condensation making the rubber warp like her was face was starting to melt.

"Hey," I said, moving aside her hair to nuzzle. A tattoo of flames etched into her neck. I traveled over them with my lips. "How did your assignment go?"

She let out a breath that disrupted her bangs.

"I take it not too well," I said, wanting to talk about what happened with Wendy McSough and her beau but I couldn't.

A bead of rubber sweat plopped into the boiling pot.

"Maybe you should take the mask off when you cook?" I said, reaching for a groove. She slapped my hand away.

"What did I tell you about touching my mask?" she said.

"It's melting into the pot."

She turned off the burner, leaned over the steam. Slowly, she removed the mask leaving it balled up on the counter. A fresh welt pulsing from her right eye.

"What happened?"

Even though she wasn't smiling, the scars from her knife made it seem as if she was.

"Who did this to you?" I pressed.

"Promise not to go crazy?"

"I won't promise anything."

"I was on assignment with Peck."

"That son-of-a-bitch," I yelled, knocking a stack of utensils to the floor.

"We had to..." She stopped, composed herself. "There are types of assignments I don't think you understand yet. We can be mercenaries."

"What do you mean?"

She stood with a hand on her hip. "What kind of wishes do you think are most popular?"

"I don't know, fucking rare objects."

A huff escaped from her mouth. "That's our cover. Like a rare diamond, yeah clients pay for that, but the real money comes from—"

"Drugs?"

"Sure, drugs. We're getting into that market, but it's not easy to crack. I'm talking about even more immoral things."

"What does this have to do with Peck?"

"I was off my game today. Don't know why. I'm on medication. Sometimes it...well, today it made me fuzzy. It's a disorder I have. Anyway, today I couldn't be off. We had a mark to take care of."

"A mark?"

"Let me finish, Errol. Please stop interrupting."

"I'm trying to understand."

"A hit. Someone we've been tasked to...*ice*. We were staking this mark out. This financier. He made bad deals with a client of ours, caused our client considerable financial distress. So he needed to be removed. We broke into his apartment and waited. Quick shot, that's usually best. The mark returned home and I collapsed. Felt my legs give out from under me. Caused a ruckus. Tipped off the mark who went running. Peck had to chase after him down the ten flights of stairs. Got him at the bottom, which wound up being convenient since there was a dumpster out the back. But Peck wasn't pleased. And he shouldn't have been. I almost ruined the whole thing."

"So he hit you?"

"It was a reaction. We were arguing outside and it just happened."

"He's hit you before?"

She shrugged one shoulder.

"Marilyn, that isn't okay. And how come I wasn't told about this side to the Card?"

"You don't have high enough clearance yet. There's a party at a club tonight. Gable was going to tell you then. Because he was pleased you notified him about Olivier and Katherine Hepburn's plans."

"Let me see it."

I inspected the bruise. Got frozen peas out of the freezer and held it to her eye. She winced but I kept it firm.

"Nothing excuses what he did," I said.

"You don't understand our relationship. Peck and I go back to the Card's inception. We were two of the first hires. The job is paramount. I would've hit him if he fucked things up."

"You never hit a woman."

"That's sexist. Anyway, it'll heal. I have thick skin."

She grabbed my arm to look at my watch.

"I should get ready. I was making a soup, but I'll take it in a thermos to go."

"C'mere."

It was so rare to see Marilyn without her mask on. I wanted to freeze the moment. I kissed her softly so as not to disrupt the frozen pea pack over her eye.

"I'm gonna take a bath, a long bath," she said. "I want to simmer."

"I can join you."

So we splashed in the tub, made a world of bubbles. Afterwards, she dressed in a red gown with a plunging neckline. She brought out a box from Bergdorf's.

"It's a suit," she said. "Gable didn't know your size, but I measured you in your sleep."

I'd never owned a full suit before. The fabric soft against my skin. Unrecognizable in the mirror to the guy I usually saw.

The party was held at a discreet location. We entered through a back alleyway in the Flatiron district. A bouncer behind a door pulled a latch that only revealed his eyes.

"What's the password?" he asked.

"Any wish fulfilled," Marilyn said.

Inside was a dim lounge. Spencer Tracy at the bar sucking down a Manhattan. Bette smoking in the corner and reapplying her lipstick. Olivier and Hepburn dancing closely to an ominous tune coming from speakers attached to the ceiling. He then spun her around and made her dip. And Peck, talking on a pay phone, yelling into the receiver but it couldn't be heard over the music.

Gable appeared out of nowhere as if he'd been conjured by a genie.

"Welcome to our little soiree," he said, shaking my hand. His cold as ice. "The last party was for show. This one is for the employees and our top clients."

A ring of people I didn't recognize sat around a circled sofa. Their eyes blinked money, you could just tell.

"Excuse me," Marilyn said. "Powder my nose."

She disappeared into a bathroom along the side.

"Happy 1979, kid," Gable said.

I tried to imagine his real face. I never had before. Guessing if he had a family, a wife and kids he was clearly neglecting. He was always around, always working. It might have been that I never really thought of him as human before, but after learning the true nature of the Card, I couldn't help but to wonder.

He pulled me in close, the mouth of his mask at my ear.

"Thank you for the information."

"About what?"

He glanced over at Olivier and Hepburn. She had her head on his shoulder, swaying lightly.

"It's nothing. Marilyn told me about the real operation by the way."

He popped a cigarette in his mouth. Struck a match out of thin air and lit.

"It was time you knew. I don't like secrets between us. Is that something you think you can do?"

I swallowed hard causing my Adam's apple to bob. Murder? None of my crimes had ever come close. But how could I say no? Saying no meant losing everything I'd worked so hard for over these last months.

"It depends," I said, confident with my answer. Under the mask, I could see his eyebrows rising for me to elaborate. "I mean, some people deserve it, right?"

"And what's your definition of 'deserve'?"

"Like there are some terrible people out there. Hitler for example, he deserved it."

"Okay, so you would ice Hitler. Good to know. What about someone who isn't responsible for killing six million?"

"Like the guy Marilyn was telling me about?"

"Precisely."

"She said he fucked up a business deal. Caused a client to lose a lot of money. So it was revenge."

"Partially. But the root of it is money."

"Isn't that the root of all evil?"

"Trite, Errol. An easy dismissal of what money can truly do. *Power*, that is what we seek."

"You mean the Card?"

"I mean everyone. We want our lives to be worthy. To have meaning. Things are unimportant. That rare diamond you delivered to Theodora Birch, she didn't want the diamond. She wanted the ability to obtain a diamond she should not possess. That is power."

"And the mark today?"

"Our client wanted to be able to erase someone who caused him much chagrin. That is power."

"So, the Card trades in power?"

"Exactly. The ability to grant wishes is the ultimate power that few will ever possess. We have some very well-known clients. You might not recognize the ones at this party, our more identifiable clients choose to remain in the shadows. Which gives me power over them. For example, when we started Richard Nixon was a client. A few years back as the Watergate scandal was ramping up, he asked us if we had the ability to make certain things disappear, to make certain people disappear. At the time, we simply obtained objects for him, rare gets. It got us thinking, or at least it got me thinking... Were we seeing our organization in too small a context?"

He eyed Olivier who began to twirl Hepburn.

"It set off a rift between Olivier and I. Olivier did not appreciate delving into the sordid. Putting his offices in Europe kept us apart, which was needed. And he handled the procurement of extraordinary finds while I took the American office to new heights. The money we brought in couldn't be farther apart. Enough for him to be jealous. See, he's as immoral as I am, but tries to establish himself as sound. He is a scorpion, his stinger primed."

Marilyn had left the bathroom and gone over to Peck. They were talking quietly at first and then started gesturing with their hands.

"He hit her, you know?"

Gable faced out his palms. "I do not get involved."

Peck grabbed her by the arm forcefully, her mouth opening in a wide O. I went go hit him, but Gable held onto my shoulder.

"Don't let her get you sucked in," he said. "You're young and could have a long future with us. She'll be your downfall if you're not smart."

Marilyn wrenched her arm away from Peck and huffed over to the bar.

"She's a big girl. She can take care of herself. Always has."

Peck went back to his call, but I wanted to murder him. Gable talked about who deserved to die, and he was a prime example.

I cooled myself down because the boss was watching. But he wouldn't always be. Even if I didn't ice Peck, I'd show him how a wonder like Marilyn should be treated. At least I'd give him a black eye to match hers.

20

AFTER THE PARTY, MARILYN WASN'T IN THE MOOD for me to come over so I got her in a cab and walked back to my folks.

I couldn't get Peck out of my mind. Imagining torturing him in various ways. Making him apologize to Marilyn and her looking at me with stars in her eyes. Solidifying our relationship even more. She'd want a type of guy who'd stand up to an asshole like Peck. That was why she told me what happened. So I'd retaliate.

When I reached my folks' block, a tall guy was leaning against the hood of a car. He wasn't smoking but his breath puffed a cloud. We made eye contact, enough for me to know I was being summoned. I thought about running off, but he knew where my folks lived so there was no use. The Errol mask had been scrunched up in my coat pocket, which told me he wasn't a member of the Card since he recognized my actual face.

He whistled and nodded at the car he leaned against. He folded himself inside the driver's side and I got in shotgun. In back, Dick Mancini spread out his arms and had lit a cigar. The car so smoky it made my eyes bleed.

"Jake," Mancini said, chewing on the cigar.

The tall guy started driving slowly, creeping along.

"Haven't heard an update about Wendy yet."

I watched Mancini though the rearview. He was so wide he practically filled out the entire backseat.

"I was gonna be in touch with you tomorrow," I said.

The tall guy flicked on the radio. "Last Dance" by Donna Summer. He kept the sound low so it could barely be heard.

"I take it you have some info," Mancini said.

"She saw her guy. He's got a leather goods store down on Eldridge Street. I followed her down."

I certainly wasn't gonna tell him that she went there because of the bug I put in her ear.

"So she's been seeing him?"

Mancini ground his cigar into an ashtray attached to the back of the seat.

"No, that's the thing. She hadn't seen him before. This was the first time."

He inched closer, breathing through his nose.

"How do you know?"

"I went into the store, listened to them. She was pissed at him for disappearing."

"Did he tell her the truth?"

I gave a quiet nod, knowing I was sealing their fate.

"And then what?"

"They were making out and went in the back room."

"That floosy," Mancini yelled. "Head downtown."

"Yes, sir," the tall guy said.

Mancini started muttering to himself. The things he'd do to them similar to my wishes for Gregory Peck. I convinced myself he was all talk. That we were headed downtown to scare her and nothing more. But when he stepped outside, he had a gun.

The front door lock was easy for the tall guy to pick. I stepped from side to side so nervous like I had to piss. I mentioned to Mancini that I could stay downstairs but he wasn't listening, too caught up in what he set out to do. The tall guy glared at me like I was an idiot and then pushed me up the stairs after Mancini.

Wendy's locks were easy to pick as well. I was really hoping they'd be impossible and Mancini would lose patience and we'd have to leave. I had to stop living in fantasies. I did that too often, relied on naivety.

Once inside her dark living room, a light pooled from the crack in her bedroom door. We heard muffled sounds that could only mean one thing. The sounds of moans and love. Of me and Marilyn. Of a headboard being slammed into a wall.

Mancini nudged the door open with his gun. I didn't want to look. I heard a scream and plugged my ears singing "Last Dance" over and over in my head to remove myself from the situation. A shot went off. A louder scream erupted.

"You killed him, you killed him," Wendy said, over and over again like a skipping record. The smell of blood tickling my nostrils. I had to hurl. I went to puke in the kitchen sink as Wendy ran out naked. We locked eyes while I wiped spittle from my mouth. She clearly knew me, but her mind was too bludgeoned with every-thing happening to precisely say how. Then a light snapped on and her face twisted in disappointment. I had sold her out like the rat I was.

Mancini lumbered from the bedroom, his gun smoking. He took his time to aim. I don't know where she was running. The tall guy stood at the door so there would be no chance for an escape. She just kind of ran around in circle, flinging her hands into the air and yelping like a wounded animal.

"Pow," Mancini said, and got her in the back of the head. She went down instantly. At least she didn't suffer. The back of her head had exploded and brain goo was flung onto the furniture. Mancini holstered his gun and sighed as if he held the plight of the world on his thick shoulders. He bent down to touch her, one last time.

"Which of you schlemiels is gonna be the one to clean this all up?" he said, and I flew over to the sink to hurl again.

21

Mancini dropped me off back by my folks with some words that "I had done good."

Then he ripped a fart and ordered the tall guy to head to the nearest titty bar. It was after midnight and I was glad no one would be up. I couldn't deal with Ma after what I'd just seen. I wanted to smoke a jay out of the window and lose myself.

I found some dried pot, rolled a joint, and took a few drags. Halfway through finishing, I was crying. Now, I wasn't a crier but these were sobs. I quickly put out the joint. On my way to the kitchen to make a sandwich, I passed by Emile's room. He wasn't asleep. I could tell by the way he was tossing and turning, although since his legs didn't really work it was more like moving his shoulders back and forth and grumbling under his breath.

"Hey, kid," I said. I called him this. He was so much younger than me I often felt like his pop. He looked up, drooling. A strand connected him to the pillow. "Hey, kid, lemme wipe that for you."

Using a handkerchief beside the bed, I wiped it away and he smiled in the way he does. It was more like a half smile.

"Can't sleep?"

He gave a soft moan.

"Yeah, neither can I. Wanna know why?"

Conversations with Emile were usually like this— one sided.

"Two people are dead because of me."

His eyes widened.

"Guy and girl. One was seeing a mob boss. Mancini. You know Mancini. The one Pop always told me to stay away from? And did I listen? No. Serves me right. So this Mancini was mad that his girl was with another guy and now they're dead. I watched the whole thing happen. He shot 'em both. Bang bang. The back of her head exploded. And then I had to clean it all up. I can still smell..."

I stopped because I thought I saw a shadow by the door.

"Ma?" I asked, but the shadow had already gone away.

"Real world shit," I said to Emile, fixing his pillow so his head wasn't slipping as bad. He thanked me with his eyes. "Anyway, forget what I said. It don't matter. Your big brother is cool. Everything is cool."

I checked in the hallway to make sure the shadow hadn't been Ma. No sign. I crept to their bedroom door but it was shut. So I went in the kitchen to make a sandwich.

I must have passed out at the dining room table over a bologna on Wonder Bread with the crusts cut off and heavy on the mayo just as I liked when I was a kid.

Morning light was coming through the blinds when Pop returned from work. His back stooped over making his limp worse. He glared at me like I was the last person he wanted to see after a long shift. He hung up his coat and gave a tired wave as he walked past.

"Pop?"

"Yeah, Jake? It was a long night."

I knew the drop off would be happen within a few days. Which meant that Georgie was gonna beat his boss's name out of him. And I was gonna help. I hadn't even figured out how it would work. I'd have to wear my Errol mask so Pop wouldn't recognize me, but if I wore the mask then Georgie and his crew would know I was working for the Card. It was all overwhelming. But if he would just tell me who his boss was, we could avoid all of this.

He strained to see me in the dim light. His eyes full of red veins.

"How was the livery car tonight?" I asked, because it was all I could think to say.

"Really? That's what you want to know?"

"No, I..." I picked up the bologna sandwich, took a sniff and realized it had gone sour. "I know that's not what you're doing."

I expected him to lash out, but he stood there like he was stoned.

"And what is it that I'm doing?"

"You're working for someone. And it's okay. Like whoever it is. But I got this feeling, Pop, that it ain't smart to be—"

"I'm gonna stop you right there." He towered over me like he did when I was a child. He could be imposing when he wanted to be. As a kid, I never wanted to piss him off. "You don't understand," he continued, almost pleading now. "You couldn't. You never will."

"Help me try."

"No. I work. I put food on the table. You're an adult and I'm still taking care of you. Your brother will never be an adult and I'll always have to take care of him. Money just goes, Jake. We never have enough. So I get two hours of sleep."

"Who are you working for? Like, maybe I can find you better work?"

I thought of him at the Card, seeing what I saw last night. Ashamed of me even more than he already was. Whoever he was working for couldn't be worse than that.

"I tried to protect you," he said, so quietly. Something he meant to keep in his head.

"Protect me from what?"

"Why are you even here? You should have your own place, but no, you did stupid things and wound up in jail. And even when you're here you don't help. You could watch Emile. You could give your ma a break. You've always been selfish."

"Pop, I can do that if you want me to. Nobody asks."

"You should do it without asking. Because you want to. Because you can see how tired we are. That good woman..."

As if she knew she was being talked about, Ma appeared from the bedroom in her nightgown looking like a ghost. Her skin so pale against the white nightgown she blended into the wall except for a flame of red hair. She observed us, disapproving of both. We lowered our heads. She held the power in this family. One glance could make us askew.

"Emile's sleeping," she said through a hushed whisper. "He's been up all night carrying on."

She looked solely at me right then. Clearly the shadow I had seen was real. Had she heard my confession?

"It's five in the morning for crissakes."

"Saoirse," Pop said, going after her but she backed up into the darkness of her bedroom. Now it was his turn to disapprove me, murder flashing in his pupils. He pointed a finger, a warning, never to bring this up again. And I wouldn't until all my worlds would inevitably collide with a terrible reckoning.

22

I wanted to see how Marilyn was doing, but when I swung by her place she wasn't there so I headed over to the card.

No Bette typing away when I arrived, which was odd. Just Olivier and Katherine Hepburn waiting. Gable wasn't in yet either.

"Looks like they're all on assignment," Olivier said. He took out a pack of his own brand of cigarettes and offered me one.

"Let me ask you," he said, after a moment of silence. "How has your introduction to the Card been?"

Hepburn swiveled in her chair to stare. Both of them sizing me up.

"It's been a few months now," I said. "Great so far I guess."

"I ask because..." Hepburn caught his eye, batted her lashes for him to continue. "It's only Katherine and I at the international office so we're actively looking for other members."

"I don't think Gable would be happy if I got poached."

"Katherine and I were going to grab lunch," he said, dominating the conversation. "Have you ever been to Le Cirque?"

I shook my head.

"No use waiting around here," Hepburn added, putting out her cigarette after one puff and heading for the door.

Le Cirque was one of those fancy establishments where the waiters called you sir. It had a giant abstract big top light shade and a glass bar with a kaleidoscope wine tower. Heavy old lady perfume filled the space coming from the various women in jewels hand-kissing one another.

"You must try the Crème Brulée," Hepburn said.

"I don't know what that is."

"You will."

I let them order for me because I could tell it gave them power. Like Gable said, power was what people craved. I'd allow them to think they could buy me.

"How often do you come to New York?" I asked.

"It's filthy," Hepburn replied, dunking her bread into a dab of oil. "Riddled with garbage and crime. I'd rather never."

"We like to check on Gable from time to time."

The waiter clearly knew both of them and they kissed on the cheeks about a dozen times. I wondered how we'd be treated with our masks still on, but no one seemed to blink. More and more it was becoming second nature. If I just saw us I would think there were three people who happened to resemble a few matinee idols.

Hepburn's aged hand went for her champagne, the veins in her neck protruding as she sipped.

"The Card is primed for greatness," Olivier said, and then observed his teeth in the reflection of a knife. "But we're not there yet."

"What will it take?"

"Good question, Errol. If I may speak frankly?"

"Please do," Hepburn said.

"We need to think about our definition of wishes. How we will be regarded. I'm not ashamed to say this is an argument Gable and I have had. I'm curious about your opinion."

"I mean, the slogan is *any* wish fulfilled..."

"Of course, but we've opened the door to the rather salacious and it's marred our clientele. In Brussels for example, that's where the international office is located, we are the purveyors of the finest things in life. That is how we are known. Royalty makes up our clients."

"Where in America it's thugs," Hepburn added. "Now that has a lot to do with the different cultures, but one is overshadowing the other. We are becoming..." She lowered her voice. "A hit man operation."

"Isn't that what pays the most?" I asked.

The waiter returned with her food. They both got a fish dish while I had a pasta with an ultra-fancy name I couldn't pronounce.

"But are we simply the pursuit of money?" Olivier asked. "When we began, sure, that was a consideration. Hobnob with the über wealthy. Gable's always had an affinity for that circle. I'm not ashamed I have as well."

"It's power you want," I said, and this perked Hepburn up. She licked her masked lips.

"Well, yes. Now let me ask you, whose world can

bring that forth? One of mobsters and hooligans or the crème de la?" Olivier asked.

"Why can't you have both?"

"When you roll in the mud with pigs..." Hepburn said.

"It's about appearances, Errol. And right now, the problem is we're being identified with those pigs. We're losing clientele."

"What does Gable think about that?"

"You can't talk to him," Hepburn said, clearly angry since she almost knocked over her champagne. "It's his way, or..."

"I know my friend very well," Olivier said. "He and I have always been at war. If it comes from me..."

"So I should tell him?"

"If you insist."

"I'm new here. I don't have any power. He's not going to listen."

Hepburn took my hand. Hers covered in liver spots and decay.

"If you would try," she said, her voice shaking. "Otherwise I fear..."

"We fear we will have to fracture, or even worse..."

"Don't say it," Hepburn said, overdramatic.

"I must," he said, lowering his head. "I feel he wants us iced."

"No, no," I said. "I never heard that. He wouldn't, especially anyone connected to the Card. We're a family."

They both cocked their heads in disagreement.

"You are young, Errol," Hepburn said. "And while youth has its advantages, you are green to the ways of business. Especially this business. He will slit our throats before he will admit to being wrong. And so therefore, we must protect ourselves."

"We must retaliate," Olivier added.

"You are not the only one we have approached," Hepburn said.

"Another member is firmly in our corner."

"Who?"

"I cannot reveal. Just know that a tide may be turning and you'll want to be on the right side," Olivier said. He finished his last bite and dabbed his lips with a napkin. "Shall we order some crème brulée?"

23

I HADN'T TALKED TO MAGGS IN A WHILE AND needed to catch up so I called him and we met downtown at McSorley's.

Gas lamps and antique newspaper clippings. An original reward for the assassination of Abraham Lincoln and Harry Houdini's handcuffs clipped to the bar. Only light or dark house brew served. We sipped and wiped the foam from off our upper lips.

"So Georgie contacted you?" Maggs asked.

I decided to go *sans* mask, mostly because Maggs hadn't been bumped up from trainee at the Card yet and I didn't want him to feel bad. Now when I wasn't wearing the mask in public, it seemed odd.

"Yeah, the bag man is dropping off a shipment in two nights. I gotta help beat the truth out of the guy. Except there's a problem."

Maggs finished his brew and ordered another.

"What's that?"

"I think my pop is the bag man."

Maggs was lucky he didn't have beer to spit out because he did a double-take.

"I'm ninety five percent certain. Didn't want to let you know until I was sure. I tried to talk to him."

"What did he say?"

"He danced around it, lashed out on me. But the bag man limped, Maggs, just like my pop."

"Hmmm, if you're there while your pop's getting interrogated, maybe you can make it easier on him?"

"That's what I'm thinking. I'd have to wear a mask though."

"Of course."

"But Georgie doesn't know we're working for the Card."

"True. You're gonna have to tell him."

"Fuck, I've been trying to figure out a way–"

"Ain't no other way. Georgie's smart, he'll know it's not worth getting on your bad side—the Card's bad side."

"I was wondering if you could tell him?"

The bartender slid down Maggs's fresh beer. Mine was running low so I ordered another one too.

"That's a big ask, man."

"Technically you've been lying to him too. And you know him better."

He ran his fingers through his hair, a nervous tell. One finger caught in a knot.

"You can say we had nothing to do with him being beaten at the end of last year. Tell him we just found out because the Card wants us to ID the bag man."

Maggs nibbled at his nails, bitten to the quick.

"I dunno, Jake. Have this rumbling in my gut that something's not gonna go right."

"That's why Georgie has to know. When you and I show up with masks, he won't be spooked. We can call him now at a pay phone outside."

We left our beers to warm and Maggs dialed Georgie who picked up after the first ring.

"Georgie here."

"Yeah, it's Maggs. Gotta sec?"

"Depends, Maggs, on what I might learn in the next sec."

"It's about the bag man we're going after."

I nodded, encouraging Maggs to continue.

"I'm with Jake right now."

I waved my hands in the air for him to stop, but it was too late.

"He needs you to know something."

I chewed my lip. "*We* need, Maggs. We need."

"Right, *we* need," Maggs continued. "So a while back we got jobs working for the Card too. We had no idea their vendetta against you. Kinda just put it all together. Georgie?"

"I'm listening."

I could hear Georgie stewing on the other line.

"So we'll be in masks when we grab the bag man, that's all I'm saying," Maggs said. "Jake in full mask because he's a regular employee, I'm still a trainee. Georgie?"

"Yeah, I'm listening. Stop saying my name."

"This is a good thing, Georgie—Sorry—We're in with the Card. We can help you."

A static buzz ate at the silence before Georgie spoke. "We'll see about that."

"We'll see you at the drop-off point," Maggs said, but Georgie had already hung up.

"What happened?" I asked.

"He hung up," Maggs said, so he did the same. "I guess he said all he had to. Do you think he sounded pissed?"

"I don't know, he's hard to read."

Back in McSorley's, the bartender had been guarding our drinks.

"Shit man," Maggs said. "Why didn't you tell Georgie before?"

"I gotta lot goin' on, Maggs. Between what's happening with my pop, and Emile too. Also, I was approached by Olivier and Hepburn."

Maggs looked quickly to the left.

"Did they approach you too?"

"No, I'm nobody. They would have no reason. But what did they want?"

"Start a war. They'd like Gable out of the picture."

"Fuck me."

"I told Gable before so he knows. He should be aware of these further developments, right?"

"I'm of the mindset that it's best to say everything you know to these bosses."

"Georgie ain't Gable. Georgie's nothing in comparison."

"Doesn't mean he ain't crazy."

"True." I took a warm, flat sip. "You wanna go to the Card now and explain everything?"

"Not really."

"Maggs, you just said–"

"No, Jake. I just called Georgie, probably got my nuts in a vice because of it. You tell Gable."

"Fuck, okay."

I left him, put my Errol mask on, and went back to

the Card. This time when I got there, Bette was pounding away at her typewriter, which meant Gable was in.

"What brings you here today?" Gable asked, after I entered his office. He was wearing a suit and working on his cuff links. "I'm headed to a gala tonight."

"It's about when I go after the bag man."

"Yes?"

"See I used to work for Georgie, odds and ends, nothing major. Like I stole him some coats. Anyway, he showed up at my folks' place wanting to make sure I'd help ID the bag man."

At the mirror, Gable fixed his square-knot tie until it hung perfectly.

"I approve of you being there. And I don't care who you used to work for."

"See, Georgie didn't know I worked for you. But now he does. I just want to be—what's the word—transparent. I don't want to keep secrets. And Maggs is with them too, he's the one who got me a job with Georgie."

"I appreciate your frankness."

I let out a breath I'd been holding in.

"I want to always be honest with you."

"How do you think this sits with Georgie?"

"I don't know him well enough. Probably not great, but what can he do? My loyalty lies with you."

"For now, he and I are working together to reveal their distributor," Gable said. "So I don't foresee a problem. But from what little I've seen, he is an impulsive man. He may decide to retaliate against us one day."

"Like I said, you have my allegiance."

"I know that..."

I heard him say "son," or at least I imagined he did.

Of course, he wouldn't. But it was the kind of assurance I needed and the fantasy was enough. He was becoming closer to a father figure than my own.

"There's one more thing," I said.

I could sense a long sigh exuding from his mask.

"I don't mean to bother."

"It's not a bother, Errol."

"Olivier and Hepburn spoke to me again."

He splashed some woodsy cologne on the mask's cheeks.

"They are trying to poach me," I said. "Get me on their side. They want to overtake the Card. Said they even had another employee of yours."

Gable remained cool and collected. No sign that this news had any bearing.

"Did they mention who?"

"No, but I can... I can help you ferret them out. I'd be happy to. Like if I hear anything."

"Yes, that would be helpful. We can keep our ears peeled."

"You don't seem–"

"Surprised?"

"Yeah, I mean I'd be after blood."

"Why do you think I brought those two traitors to the States right now? I already knew."

"Really?"

"I'm always twelve steps ahead, Errol. Guarantee."

He playfully slapped my cheek, the tang of his cologne lingering.

"Now if you will excuse me?"

"Oh, right, right."

"A gala awaits," he said, donning a top hat and tipping it my way. "Ah, the many hats I wear."

24

Maggs and I waited in Georgie's van with our masks on. Georgie driving and Jack with the Nose outside by the drop-off point smoking cigarettes down to the filter. The smartest bet would be to defuse the situation once we nabbed Pop. Make him understand that giving up his boss was tantamount to him staying alive.

Georgie switched on the radio and of course "Stayin' Alive" by the Bee Gees started playing as if it knew what was about to occur. I hated the fucking Bee Gees. I wish I was born into a different generation that didn't give a flying rat's ass about Disco.

After waiting for about half an hour and going through some of Disco's worst top hits, a garbage truck banged down the street and Pop slowly stepped out. He wore a stocking over his face, but still limped like he usually did. Georgie put the van in drive and we crawled closer to their meeting. Pop held a bag filled with the supposed drugs while Jack with the Nose carried an empty one. They made the switch. As Pop limped away, Georgie gunned it and the van swept beside Pop. We flung open the doors and yanked him inside. Then Jack with the Nose hopped in as well. We closed the doors and drove off along the West Side Highway out of the city where there would be less cars around.

"What the fuck is going on?" Pop yelled, a mix of anger and fear in his voice. I rarely heard him be scared of anything before, but I could tell. He wanted to seem tough but was quivering.

Jack with the Nose went through the bag Pop had handed over. Bricks of cocaine, the purest I'd ever seen. None cut with baking soda for whoever sniffed these.

"Who do you work for?" Maggs asked, shaking Pop.

"My back," was all he could say, grimacing.

"Listen," I said, and his ears perked up. Did he recognize my voice? I tried to lower and make it sound more threatening. "We don't want to hurt you, we just need to know your boss."

His eyes shot toward the window. An almost full moon hung outside. The smell of the Hudson River rushing in. He was stalling, trying to figure out his next move.

"Tell us!" Maggs said, grabbing him by the collar.

Jack with the Nose whipped a pistol out of his inside pocket and stuck it in Pop's face. A hint of urine filled the van and I wondered if Pop wet himself.

"We aren't messing around, ya-hear," Jack said. "If you don't tell us what we want to hear, we dump you in the bottom of the river."

"Please," I said, begging. Behind my mask, tears emerged. I was thankful that the mask kept them hidden.

"I'm dead either way," Pop said, defeated.

"No, we can protect you," I said, altering my voice. Jack with the Nose shot me a look like I was crazy. "Your boss can't hurt you because he won't be around anymore."

Now Georgie eyed me in the rearview mirror. One eyebrow raised in suspicion.

"Can your boss say the same thing?" I asked. "We work for a very high-powered organization. Your boss has been stepping on the turf of our distributor. You are just a middle man—"

"Where are you taking me?" he cried. "I can't breathe."

I nodded to Maggs to take the stocking off his head. Pop looked so old once it was removed. A tiny confused man. His hair stood up from his scalp in a state of shock. He really couldn't catch his breath.

"Sit up," I said. "Elevate your head."

I got him to a sitting position, propping him back against the van wall.

"Calm down, deep breaths," I said.

"We don't have time for this," Jack with the Nose said, cocking his gun.

I bashed Jack with the Nose with my elbow. "You ain't running this, motherfucker. I am. Do you understand? Give me the gun."

Jack with the Nose was hesitant, but Georgie gave him the okay. He passed over the gun and I handed it to Maggs.

"No one is gonna shoot you, man," I said to Pop. "But you have to give us what we want. Once you say the name, that person will vanish. My boss will make sure of it."

His eyes clocked from me to Maggs, over to Jack with the Nose, and back to me.

"Don't be scared. You have my word you'll be protected."

I knew that to make this happen, I'd have to tell Gable how Pop was involved. But Gable would be so pleased I got a name, I was certain he'd watch over Pop.

"He's a local mobster," Pop said. He looked again at the almost full moon as if it could give him answers. "Someone I owed money to a long time ago who never let me out of my debt. He's a vile person and I'd spit on his grave if you killed him."

"It's okay, man," I said, I was rubbing his shoulder, putting him at ease. I would have hugged him if I could, anything to bring out the truth.

"Name's Richard Mancini, but he goes by Dick. Runs things out of Hell's Kitchen."

I should have known. And honestly when he revealed this, I was less shocked than I thought I'd be. Pop wanted Dick to stay away from hiring me because all this time he'd been under Dick's thumb. He knew what Mancini was capable of doing.

For the others, this name meant nothing. Maybe they'd heard of him since Dick had a legacy in the Hell's Kitchen scene, but he was a two-bit mobster like a million other guys. He wasn't engrained in their family. They also didn't know he was a client of the Card.

I remembered something Gable had said. That he was always twelve steps ahead—guaranteed. He had to have an inkling that Mancini was the one cutting in on his own distributor's turf. Gable might not have had actual proof, and to make a big move he would need it, but this had all been set up from the get-go. I wondered if he knew how Pop was involved as well. If I'd been hired originally because of my connection. He warned that there should never be secrets between members of the Card. I took him for a truthful man and would give him the benefit of the doubt. But I had a sinking feeling that the world was a big game of chess for him and I was just a pawn, we all were.

"Toss him out," Georgie said, while Andy Gibb hit a high note over the radio.

"While we're moving?" I asked.

"He's of no use to us."

"Slow down."

"What was that?"

"Slow the fuck down," I said, grabbing the gun from Maggs and sticking it in the back of Georgie's skull.

"All right, all right," Georgie said, and found a turn-off where we pulled over to the side. Maggs slid open the door and I gave Pop a gentle push out. He tumbled onto the grass, the door slammed, and we drove away.

Through the back windows, I could see him rise on shaky feet and brush off the dirt from his uniform. He wasn't staring at us, but locked on the moon, asking it for a hint of what his troubled future may hold.

25

BACK AT THE CARD'S OFFICES, MARILYN WAS IN
the waiting area arguing with Bette.

They stopped when I came inside. Maggs had gone
back with Georgie and Jack with the Nose. I was done
with Georgie's racket. I didn't owe him anything and
was firmly working for the Card, but I needed to know I
wasn't being used as bait.

"You look like you had a run in with a ghost,"
Marilyn said.

"How can you tell through the mask?"

"The mask starts to wear you after a while," she
said. "Telegraphing emotions. That's the point. So you
eventually become Errol, or Marilyn, or even Bette."

Bette plopped down at her desk and began
hammering away at the keys.

"Are you typing this conversation?" I asked.

"No," Bette said. "Only what Marilyn and I were
just discussing."

"I was being a doll and told her to watch out,"
Marilyn said.

"And I said, I didn't need her concern."

"How's that bruise of yours doing?" Marilyn asked.

"It's the colors of the rainbow," Bette said.

"He's a son-of-a-bitch."

"You only say that because he isn't yours anymore."

"I wouldn't get back with him if he was the last dick on Earth."

"Ladies," I said, stepping in. "I have to speak to Gable. It's important. Is he in?"

"You know where the door is," Bette said, and went back to typing.

As much as I wanted to be there for Marilyn by antagonizing Bette, I didn't have the time. In Gable's office, he was on the phone. The kind of conversation where someone spoke a lot and you just listened on the other end. I could hear the voice was Spanish, speaking very fast. The voice was not pleased.

Gable held up his finger, speaking Spanish back in a calm tone. Nothing rattled him. I was on edge. I'd inhaled six cigarettes outside before I came up, my tongue on fire.

"*Adios*," Gable finally said, the only word I understood. He hung up the phone. "I should be a fireman since I'm so good at putting out fires. Sometimes I feel it's all I do."

"Well, I helped put out one just now."

He went to the bar and tapped some bourbon in two glasses.

"Dick Mancini," I said, waiting for a reaction. Like usual, he gave none.

"What about him?"

"The bag man's boss. After threatening the guy's life, he gave up a name. Said he'd been in debt with

Mancini for a long time. I don't blame the bag man. In fact, I said we would try to protect him."

"The bag man isn't my concern, but bravo, Errol Flynn."

"Did you know?"

"What's that?"

"About Mancini. Did you know he was the distributor?"

He sucked back his drink. "Yes. Well, ninety percent certain. It's a cliché to keep your enemies close, but it works well. I wanted eyes on him."

"And now?"

"What if I said that *you* will kill him?"

I nearly dropped the drink, imagining it shattering on the floor, flinging glass into the air until we were sliced to pieces. But I took Gable's strategy of not showing my inner turmoil.

"Why me?"

"You were bumped up from trainee, but you are not an operative until you've shed blood. That's the rule. Those two girls outside, Gregory Peck, Spencer Tracy, they've all erected tombstones."

"I had a feeling–"

"Wouldn't Dick Mancini be someone you wanted gone anyway?"

"I... Now why would you say that?"

He poured another drink, brought it to his lips. "Because of what he's done to your family. To your father."

The room got slanty, a dizzy spell taking over. I looked down at my drink to see if it was the culprit. But Gable had drunken from the same bottle.

"What do you know about my pop?"

"Louis Barnum, garbage man, livery driver, married to Saoirse, two children, you and Emile who has severe disabilities. I know that your father has spent way too much money on doctors that have never pinpointed your brother's issue. When he was born, your father worked for Dick Mancini, all the money he earned going to medical bills. So much so that he owed Mancini more than he brought in. And so, Mancini made him his bitch."

I wanted to slug him from calling Pop that but refrained myself.

"Settle down, Errol."

Even though I'd tried to maintain, the anger was clearly spilling out my pores.

"I'm not the enemy here. I am the savior. For if you get rid of Mancini, the biggest threat to your family, you will also get the promotion here you so desire."

"And if I don't kill him?"

"Another operative will, and I will have lost my faith. But I know you will comply."

"How so?"

"We are so alike, Errol. I see much of myself in you, or at least, who I used to be when I was young and hungry. I have been very impressed."

"But you've been setting all this up like some game."

"It's far from a game, Errol. But you are right in some ways. I maneuver pieces around to get the desired outcome. To ensure what I want comes true. That is all. I was not deceiving you. I was holding onto information you didn't need to know yet. You had to come to that revelation on your own."

The dizziness wound down, the room slanting back to normal.

"I was gonna tell you how my pop was connected," I said, finishing the drink.

"I know you were. And he will be protected. Mancini has goons that won't be pleased, but they are no match. You can assure him his safety."

"He doesn't know what I do."

"He does now. And better that you two don't have secrets between you anymore. There have been many revelations tonight."

"How do you want Mancini killed?"

He snapped his fingers. "That's more like it. Get to the meat, the heart. We ice him tomorrow morning when he goes to get his newspaper. He always has a cigar at his door, pacing around for a few minutes, wife and kids still asleep, the block quiet. He won't see it coming."

Gable sucked up the last drop of bourbon through his teeth.

26

On an unseasonably warm winter's morning, I took my first life.

I didn't sleep the night before, the adrenaline and hesitation keeping my heart pounding. I left my folks' place in the pre-dawn dark. The city empty. The past snow turned to dirty slush. Graffiti tags along our neighborhood walls. Half-empty bottles hugging the curb. I had a gun and a knife concealed in my inside pockets. The gun proving a challenge because I was far from a tested shot and it would cause a bang. Lights would appear in windows. Some old lady threatening she'd call the cops. The knife silent but just as deadly.

I waited an hour behind a parked car watching Dick Mancini's front stoop. His family lived in the entire three-story building, a rarity for the neighborhood, most of us squeezing too many kids into cramped spaces. The lights remained off in his home, curtains drawn. Around five a.m., a newspaper boy bicycled along and tossed a fresh paper at his doorstep. The paper knocked against the door, and I heard the sound of a dog mewling.

From across the street, I had a pretty clean shot. But my hand was shaking like mad. If I missed, he'd run back inside, maybe even get out his own gun and fire. The knife made the most sense. I crossed the street and crouched behind a parked car a few feet from the doorsteps. The dog started mewling louder and Mancini's heavy feet pounded down the stairs. The door swung open.

He was in a bathrobe with a wifebeater and pajama bottoms with slippers. The bathrobe tied under his gut, supporting it well. He popped a cigar in his mouth, cut the head off and lit, sucking in the smoke and exhaling before he'd inhale. I smoked a cigar wrong my first time, which led to vomiting up a ham sandwich.

I slid the knife out of my inside pocket. The sun was peeking through the darkness and the blade flashed a show of light. Run past, jab Mancini twice in the stomach, then go for his throat. That was how I planned. After that, I'd never be the same person again. For twenty-four years, I'd never killed a man, but that would change. Hell would be waiting.

But a world without Dick Mancini was surely a better place. How many men like Pop had he threatened? Many likely wished him dead. As an operative for the Desire Card, I aimed to make those wishes come true. Not only that, but Pop would be free. I'd never discuss it with him. It'd be this unsaid thing between us, but he'd know I saved the family. And as a full operative, I'd be making the kind of money that could really help Emile's condition.

So I observed Mancini sucking the final cigar of his

life. He had no idea this morning would be his last. It was crazy to imagine the power I held right then. Here this boss thought he had the power, but he had none. He'd never see it coming. He would never even understand what happened and why. For I wore my Errol Flynn mask remaining incognito.

Mancini bent down to the pick up the paper. The lead stories showed that Ayatollah Ruhollah Khomeini returned to Tehran. And former Sex Pistols bassist, Sid Vicious, was dead at twenty-one of a heroin overdose in New York City after being released from a fifty-five-day sentence at Rikers Island prison on bail. I wished it was John Travolta or the Bee Gees or some other lame Disco band rather than Sid from the Sex Pistols. The headline tomorrow would be Mancini's death, although it might not even make the front page. I'd heard about the grumblings of an Iranian Revolution about to take place that could dwarf local news like Mancini. A big man like him not as big as he thought.

Mancini perused the cover page, likely not caring about Sid Vicious or the Ayatollah. His fat thumbs turned to an inside story, moving his cigar from one side of his mouth to the other with his tongue. His dog then paddled out, a Shih Tzu with a wagging tail that pissed against a fire hydrant.

"Good doggie, good doggie," he said, patting his massive thigh.

Now I would strike. His attention caught between his dog, the paper, and a cigar. Like a ninja I whisked down the street, brandishing my blade and stabbing him twice in the stomach. He was so fat I wondered if I even hit an organ or if he was buffered by blubber. Blood started pooling out and he dropped the newspaper and the cigar flew from his mouth. The little Shih Tzu yapped and I nudged it away with my foot while I gave Mancini an uppercut with the blade.

"This is for my pop," I said, staring into his bulging eyes. A spurt of blood dribbled from his lips. He reached out to choke me but death took hold and he flopped face first on the pavement. The Shih Tzu scurried around him, licking up the blood, yapping to the sky. I ran off as a light in the window turned on. From down the block, I could see the curtains part and his wife Charlotte in curlers stick out her head and shriek to the heavens. I turned the corner, and then another, and another until I couldn't hear her anymore. I dropped the bloody knife down a drainpipe, removed the mask, and whistled as I hit Broadway and melded in with the crowd.

I'd be lying if I said it wasn't the most thrilling few minutes of my short life.

27

Running on pure adrenaline, I made it to Marilyn's place with the intent on fucking.

Not making love, no caresses, pure animals. I was charged. Like I'd been plugged in, electricity coursing through my veins instead of blood. She'd just gotten out of the shower, a towel around her chest. She didn't shower with her mask, one of the few times she kept it off. She reached for it but I wouldn't let her. We hadn't fucked as Jake and... and... and I realized I never knew her real name. While she splayed on the bed and I ground on top of her, I asked "Who are you, Marilyn?"

She shut her eyes, screamed "harder, harder, harder," scratched my back with her long nails until she drew blood. "I'm Marilyn," she said, tears building. "Please, that's all I ever want to be."

Afterwards we smoked cigarettes while still in the sheets. She'd put the mask back on, smoothed it down so it blended with her face. I kissed her famous mole.

"It's been so long since I've been someone else," she said. "I'm not that person anymore."

"I understand."

"I don't think you do. We're still so different, Errol. Our experiences. You didn't come from pain. You haven't experienced hurt and death like I have."

I propped myself up on my elbow. "You can tell me some time."

She shrugged one delicate shoulder. "Maybe. One day."

"And death, I've seen it up close. I killed someone this morning."

Her fake smile seemed to widen to cartoonish proportions. "Who?"

"Dick Mancini. A mob boss. The guy who was overstepping his bounds on our client's turf."

"Does Gable know?"

"I called it into Bette on my way over."

She frowned at the mention of Bette. Their relationship souring even more than before.

"How did it feel?"

I thought of the rush. Mancini's blood gushing. His body falling. The transfer of energy as it left Mancini and soared into me.

"Exhilarating," I said, oddly proud of myself.

"My first was a few years ago," she said, relishing in the past. "A mark Gable had picked just for me. Pure revenge kill. This guy who had stolen millions from the company he worked for. Our client demanding an icing. I met the mark at a hotel bar. He was already two drinks in. Thought I was a hooker, and I let him be foolish. Flirted my way up to his room. I wanted to ice him mid-coitus. He was handsome, I remember that. I would have iced him earlier if he wasn't. But it thrilled me to know I was the last pleasure he'd have. Pleasure before the pain. That's power. I rode him like a cow girl and orgasmed when I wrapped a wire around his neck. He probably thought I was being kinky. He had this *huh, huh, huh* kind of laugh. 'Huh, huh, huh, what are you doing, girl? 'I'm killing you,' I said. And he kept *huh, huh, huh-ing*. But then I pulled tight, cut off his air. His face puffing up, shades of blue and purple. Arms flailing out. He was big, but I'm strong. I clamped my thighs to keep him in place. He struggled and we flopped around like we were still fucking, but he was dying. Transferring of energy like you said. I stole his, swam in it, licked up every last drop. Delicious. He tasted like pure gold. Left him on the bed with his tongue dangling from his mouth, the blood from the wire soaking the sheets. Took his watch, the cheesy necklace he wore, his money clip. Keep them all in a tiny box under my bed. A reminder. When I turned. When I allowed the shape shifter within me to be born."

She cackled, the laughs never-ending. I laughed along too with her in my arms.

"Thank you," I said.

She was shy and glanced away. "For what?"

"For all of this. Allowing me into the Card's world."

"It's all you, baby. I simply made the introduction, you made it happen."

"Still, if not for you...?"

"Maybe, but I believe in fate. Like this would be your fate even without me. You were destined to find the Card."

"Do you think Gable will make me an operative now?"

"Pretty much guaranteed. You've proved yourself in every way. I'm so proud, my baby."

She rubbed her stomach, and I imagined her pregnant with my child. A family we would create. Leaving this miserable city eventually and getting a place in the suburbs. Taking the train in for missions and returning to our paradise at night. A boy and a girl, a dog named Skip, neighbors that waved hello. I was already going to hell so I might as well have as much heaven on Earth as possible. The kids growing up and leaving for college. Marilyn and I getting old on a porch swing. But would we ever get old with the masks? We'd stay youthful forever, just like it should be.

"What are you thinking?" she said, running a finger up and down my worry lines.

"Our future."

Her face stayed still. I'd notice that at times. If she didn't make the effort, a glazed over expression would appear.

"Did I say too much?" I asked, my heart twisting in my chest.

"No, no, just... A future? I never really thought of the future before. I'm trying to make it through every day."

"You can. With me. You can wish for anything you want."

Now her face lit up. "Any wish fulfilled?"

She rolled over and a popped a few prescription pills. "For my headaches," she said. I didn't question. She touched my cheek. "You're beautiful."

"Stop," I said, never being called that before.

"You are. You would never hit me."

"Why would you even say that?"

"Because it's all the love I know."

"Never again."

I scooped her up, lay on top, felt our hearts beating against each other. We kissed, her tongue chalky from the pills but still somehow sweet. I didn't know what time it was and didn't care. It was probably the happiest moment of my life. But with great highs come the inevitable downfalls. They would take a while to really destroy our bliss, but when they'd arrive, we wouldn't stand a chance. This perfect bubble popped with no regard. What else did I really deserve? I should've known that when you make a deal with the devil himself, he only takes and takes until there'd be nothing left but bones and dust.

28

1979 SURE WAS A WHIRLWIND.

It came and went with pop and flair, dead bodies
and despair. I killed a man for every season. Made it to
operative status in what Gable called record time.
Mancini's icing put me there. Now it would be a test to
see who'd become Gable's station agent, his number
two. Marilyn and Peck in line for the job, but they were
older and more seasoned, more complacent. And while
I'd be happy if it was her, if Peck was promoted, I'd ice
him for the spot.

I moved in permanently with Marilyn. Things had
gotten pretty bad between Pop and I after the van incident. While we never spoke of it, I knew he knew. His
embarrassment plus his disappointment in my life
choices made it easier to stay apart. Also, Ma had been
suspicious of my new job too. She didn't come out and
ask directly, but she sure hinted. And between that and
the occasional disapproving glance, I chose Marilyn's
crib.

I felt bad for leaving Emile, but I couldn't let the kid

dictate my life. There'd be a lot less yelling and uncomfortable silences without me there. Besides, what twenty-four-year-old guy still lived with his folks? It was getting pathetic.

Living with Marilyn was a dream, at least at first. In the beginning of our relationship, we were our best selves. The phony façade. I never picked the wax from my ears around her. She never pooped. We put on our masks and smiled the whole way. But things were bubbling underneath. I didn't like the amount of time she spent with Peck, even though they were just working together. Gable like them to team up on assignments, but Marilyn always seemed so dour when she'd return. I could tell it was affecting her. She came home one night in late February when we were supposed to watch the partial solar eclipse and went in the bathroom and didn't come out until morning. I learned it was best to leave her when she got in her moods. The Norma Jean side of her personality. Manic and sometimes sad. It made me sad too, but I wanted to respect her wishes.

I started to see Maggs less too. On the day the nuclear power plant exploded on Three Mile Island, Gable pulled me into the office and told me he was cutting ties with Maggs. "It's not a good fit," was all he said. Later on, Maggs longed to know why but I couldn't give him answers, even if I knew them. He got jealous because Georgie's crew wasn't really bringing in money after getting out of the drug trade and he had to take up another job at a different Nedicks. I once passed by his new employment and saw him pouring a cup of stale coffee and looking like he wished he could end his life. It got so depressing I stopped hanging around him. It was the first time we drifted apart. Since I was so busy, I didn't really notice too much.

I killed my second man on April 10th, a news day devoted to a tornado that killed forty-two people in Wichita Falls, Texas, the most notable of the twenty-five other tornados that day. God wiped out land and lives with a swoop of his hand while on a smaller scale I choked a cheating husband who stepped out on his wife and kids one too many times. Mancini's icing was easy to justify. Icing a guy who couldn't stop sticking his dick into every vagina out there proved more difficult to explain to myself. I got real depressed—Marilyn kind of depressed. I shut myself in the bathroom like she had done and found her vial of pills in the medicine cabinet. I took three and experienced loopy hallucinations, wound up with my finger down my throat over the toilet. Crawled into bed and didn't emerge until the sun rose and Marilyn returned. She found me curled up in a ball with puke along my cheek and got me in a shower and washed away all my blues. She kissed the bruises the guy I killed gave me. She said how proud Gable was. And it was true. I hadn't been bumped up to station agent yet, but I was close.

Olivier and Katherine Hepburn returned to Europe without the identity of their mole being revealed. Gable said that it wasn't time for war...yet. That in the art of war you waited for your enemy to make a mistake first. Gable could be patient. I had some minimal communication with them over the year, but nothing more than business transactions until eventually the idea of them striking Gable faded into the background.

On the day the Rangers lost the Stanley Cup, I killed my third person. The reason was never given. He was very old and a hoarder living up in Harlem. His apartment filled with stacks of records and books. It smelled like dust and death. All I had to do was turn his gas on and slip a sleeping pill into his milk. He never knew I was there. A day later, he made the six-o'clock news. He had no family, no one to claim his body. There was no funeral. I wondered why such a ghost of a person would have a hit on him, but I knew never to ask Gable. You received assignments at the Card, you never questioned them. But for each icing, I made a mark on my body. I'd heat up a fork and touch it to the inside of my wrist until a red line formed. The memory of who I'd become.

It wasn't all doom and gloom. There were lavish parties at Café Un Deux Trois in Midtown, front row seats at the Yankees with Billy Martin walking right by our noses, US Open tickets for a Jimmy Conners match, a birthday party at Park Tavern restaurant and a premiere showing of *Apocalypse Now* at the Regency, drinks at Joe Allen and the Lion's Head, lunch at the Plaza, and cocaine... lots and lots of cocaine.

The client who wanted Mancini out of the picture began using us as a distributor. He was definitely based out of the States, likely South America. His identity shrouded in mystery. The amount of blow we delivered that year kept the entire island of Manhattan wired. We were *the* go-betweens, and I went to bed each night high on sheets of money. So I started tooting a lot too. It went with the territory. Marilyn did as well. We'd do a line when we'd wake, a line before an assignment, a line to keep the night going into morning. We barely slept. I remember watching when Etan Patz was kidnapped in the city, the "Boy on the Milk Carton," hours and hours of speculation as to who took him. I had my theories. I smoked cigarettes to the filter and rubbed my gums while glued to the tube until Marilyn would finally come home and lure me to bed. They never solved his crime.

When the Sony Walkman first came out in Japan, Gable was able to procure it as a present for each of us. I'd bop around the city listening to Springsteen's "Born to Run." One time I saw Cheryl. She was walking with Crazy Eddie and visibly pregnant. I was high and halfway through "Jungleland." She seemed miserable. Crazy Eddie was obviously stepping out on her and she was about to pop. She looked ten years older than she had when I saw her last. She went to wave. I pretended not to see her and she lowered her hand blushing. Even more pathetic, I saw she was still wearing the tennis bracelet I'd stolen from Tiffany's.

In August, we went to Studio 54 and danced to Michael Jackson's *Off the Wall*. He was there in a felt hat and track suit with Liza Minelli. It was the first time I'd actually liked Disco music. My last icing of the year was the day Pope John Paul arrived in New York City to speak to the U.N. This icing was a diplomat in town. The diplomat liked to walk along the FDR at night and smell the East River. I pushed him over, watched him flail his arms and yell for help, but the October waters were too cold and his body went into shock. Again, I never asked who set up his demise.

In November, the world was shocked when the Iran Hostage Crisis began and fifty-three Americans were taken hostage by radicals who demanded that the U.S. send the former Shah of Iran back to trial. At the Card's office, we watched the whole saga play out like a family would. Marilyn actually wept for the hostages while Bette filed her nails and Peck cracked jokes. The phone rang and it was our number one client, the drug supplier from South America. I'd heard about Pablo Escobar and began to wonder if it was him. Gable seemed to know such high-powered people it wasn't impossible. He took the call in his office and came out beaming. The client would be in Miami at the beginning of next year where we'd set up the next stage of our partnered operation.

Throughout November, we held off on too many new wishes while we developed the biggest one about to hit the Card. Having time off, I did a lot of cocaine and watched the Iran Hostage Crisis play out. President Carter froze all Iranian assets. The Ayatollah then released thirteen female and Black hostages. I got a cassette tape of Pink Floyd's *The Wall* and my mind zoomed to new territories. I lived in the music, a soundtrack to my every moment. 1979 was hurtling to a close as we'd celebrate the emergence of a brand-new decade by renting out the entire Barbetta restaurant for the night.

I slapped on my headphones and headed to the theater district, snapping my fingers along to the song "The Thin Ice" on *The Wall*.

29

BARBETTA WAS FANCY AS HELL.

Humungous chandeliers hanging from the ceiling, candelabras, and the feel of stepping into the home of Louie XV. Gable had rented out the whole place, not cheap but he liked to swing his dick around in terms of what the Card could now afford. The mystery client was paying off and taking the Card to new heights.

I scanned the place for Marilyn but she hadn't arrived yet. She and Peck out on assignment. Wishes didn't stop just because it was New Year's. I caught up with Spencer Tracy who was sampling some meatballs in cream sauce. He'd stuff one in his face before he was able to finish chewing, his cheeks puffed out like a hamster.

"These are good," he said, offering his plate.

"Have you seen Marilyn?"

He shook his head. "She's probably on her way with Peck."

I must've been making a face through my mask

because he put down his meatballs to squeeze my shoulder.

"They're not fucking," he said.

"I wasn't—"

"Yes. You were."

"What do you think of Peck?" I asked, and he didn't answer right away. It was hard to know who I should remain loyal to at the Card—Marilyn certainly—but the others a blur. I had little relationship with Bette, and she was doing Peck. I'd never speak bad about another operative to Gable, but Spencer Tracy seemed like fair territory.

He jammed his pinky in his ear, picked out some wax and observed.

"What are you asking?"

I lowered my voice. "Whether he can be trusted."

"Can any of us?"

"Yes. I can."

"Marilyn and Peck were Gable's first two hires. They are engrained in the Card." Through the mask, his eyes flitted back and forth. "You should be careful how you speak."

"I didn't mean—"

"Yes. You did."

He picked up his plate of meatballs and began stuffing them in his mouth again. "Relax and enjoy the party."

He slipped away as I heard "Ring My Bell" take over the stuffy classical music playing before. Unlike last year, there were a lot of clients I recognized. A TV star, a model, a CEO, a politician and his wife, an artist who painted while nude and used her body on the canvas, a film director of a movie I recently saw, a writer who hit the *Times* bestseller list. I was taught to not reveal any of their names. At the party, they all wore masks to remain incognito but I could tell who they were.

Bette danced by herself in the corner with a cigarette between her lips. Every time the chorus was sung, she came alive and rung an imaginary bell. She was wearing flared blue bell bottoms and a paisley blouse, her hair feathered as if Bette Davis was a girl in her twenties in 1979. Not having learned from my interaction with Spencer Tracy, I sidled up to Bette and began dancing too. Now, I was a pretty good dancer. I had moves. But she acted like I was a ghost. "Ring My Bell" switched to "Heart of Glass" by Blondie. Blondie was okay. The song kind of sounded like glass and the coke was fully kicking in. I started carrying a thimble of candy cane in a necklace. "Wanna bump?" I asked her. She shrugged but I could tell she did. I tapped some out on my finger and held it under her nose. She gave a look like it was a slug but snorted it up anyway, mouthing the words to the song.

"Have you heard from Peck?" I asked, and I could see a frown appear in her mouth hole. She didn't answer. "How do you feel about how much time he spends with Marilyn?"

Okay, I was jealous. I never got to do assignments with Marilyn, and Peck got her all day. Whenever I'd question about it, she said I didn't have that kind of clearance. I wasn't sure if I was more curious about what they were doing or the fact that they were doing it together. I started to dream about them. Oftentimes, Marilyn didn't come home at night, dragging herself through the door by morning. Once she seemed like she'd been hit again, but she brushed it off. When you look at the profile of someone wearing a mask, you can see their true face through a quarter of an inch space in their eye hole. Her left eye clearly bruised, practically closed shut and purple. She swore she'd bumped into a low hanging beam, but I didn't buy it. Especially because that day Peck had this smug look to him. Like he had power over her. I wanted to kick his fucking ass.

Dancing with Bette, when she turned to show her profile, the same eye appeared swollen over. She caught me noticing and pivoted to the other side. I grabbed her arm and marched her away from the dance floor.

"Let go of me," she shrieked, the music too loud for anyone to hear. I pulled her into a closed-off room with two tiny pink chairs and a sofa in between. Wooden walls with gold etchings. Three tiny floral plants in pots. "Heart of Glass" muffled.

"What did he do to you?"

She shook out of my grip. "Fuck you. Who do you think you are?"

From her cleavage, she pulled out a pack of cigarettes, flipped one between her lips and lit.

"Your eye."

"I walked into–"

"A low hanging beam," I yelled. "Is that what he told you to say? Marilyn had the same bruise last month."

"Did she?" Bette asked, a hint of jealousy in her tone. "Well then, she asked for it."

I could've hit her. I had to hold my fists back. I was becoming no better than Peck.

"She would never."

"The relationship they used to have," Bette said,

coughing a laugh. "Some kinda twisted. Bled for each other. Literally."

"What do you mean?"

"Use and abuse. I told you that's what your girl likes. Why you'll never be enough."

"We're just fine."

"Then why you in here with me?" She took a hard suck, spit out the smoke. "I know the kind of guy Peck is and I'm okay with it. So I'm less pathetic than you."

"You're the definition of pathetic."

"At least I'm not the last to know..."

"The last to know *what*?"

She licked her lipsticked lips. "The last to know her secret."

I got in her face. "You better stop talking in riddles."

She exhaled in my eyes, blurring it all. They burned, forming tears. It was an excuse to cry and let it all out.

"Your lovely girl is with child," she said.

She gave a hard push, sending me back onto one of the pink chairs.

"And now comes the bigger question," Bette said. "Is the little babe yours?"

The muffled sounds of "Heart of Glass" came to an end, replaced with the Bee Gee's "Tragedy."

30

WITH A MIX OF MOURNING THE LOSS OF MY YOUTH and the delight of possibly becoming a new father, I wandered back to the party and went right for a tray of champagne.

After sucking down two, I felt more at ease. But then suspicions began to sink in. Why hadn't Marilyn told me? She hated Bette and yet Bette had found out before me. I figured I was the hardest person to tell, which meant that Marilyn may not decide to keep it. Abortion just became legal a few years ago, and I needed to respect it as her choice. We'd have a good talk and I'd lay out my plans to get us out of this filthy city and up to the suburbs to begin our family. I also couldn't believe it wasn't mine.

Swiveling around, I bumped right into Katherine Hepburn. She was made up of practically just bones, and I nearly knocked her to pieces. I didn't expect to see her, knowing I hadn't been updated about Gable's plan for her and Olivier.

"I'm sorry," I said. She had spilled a drink over her

blouse and was mopping it up with the tiniest napkin in existence. She seemed older, frailer than I remembered.

I nabbed a handful of napkins from a waiter passing by and tried to dab away the stain.

"It's no use," she said. "I'm already dead."

"What?"

"I said the stain is red." She pointed to wine spreading across the fabric.

"I thought you said–"

"Darling," Olivier said, coming to her aid with a silk handkerchief.

She was in tears now, her body quivering.

"Dear, take it to the bathroom," he said, motioning toward a door off to the side. She gathered her soaked napkins and shuffled away. "Hasn't been the same for some time."

"What's wrong with her?"

Olivier looked at me carefully, as if I was a moron. "You know."

"I don't."

"We've both been marked." His lips close to my ear, he continued. "*You* told on us."

"Gable already knew."

"Did he? Or did he simply tell you that?"

He took a sip of his Manhattan, swirled the liquor around, and then dove in for another.

"Why are you here then?" I asked, my tone saying *he* was the moron this time.

"We've been summoned."

"And you do whatever you're told?"

"We'd be found wherever we went. There's no escaping–"

Like he knew we were discussing him, Gable appeared gnawing on a bloody piece of steak.

"Errol, I didn't see you enter."

I'd been busy, I wanted to say but he could read it all over my face.

"Just got here," I said, my eyes dancing around. "Really great spot."

"It's a New York institution. Their steak is fabulous." He speared a piece from his plate and directed it my way. I plucked it off his fork and into my mouth. Rare in the center, hot and dripping with blood.

"Good," I said, giving a thumbs up.

"And how was your flight?" Gable asked, placing the plate down to put his arm around Olivier.

"Rocky." Olivier jingled his ice. "Much turbulence."

"Ah, sorry to hear. And where's Katherine?"

"In the bathroom. She spilled wine on herself."

"I knocked into her," I said.

"Yes... Errol is responsible." He knocked back the swill at the bottom of the glass. "I should check on her."

Before Gable could answer, Olivier sulked off.

"We're making our move," Gable said, under his breath. "Before they leave town again. First her, then we'll see about him."

"Of course."

"They are planning to ice me. I've heard word from across the pond. They have a mole but so do I. I shouldn't have waited this long."

"How are you planning on doing it?"

"The stroke of midnight. When everyone is distracted."

I was about to ask if he meant for me to do the deed.

"Spencer Tracy's already on it."

I let out a spurt of relieved breath. Between that and having to talk to Marilyn about our planned future would be too much.

"Just Katherine?"

Gable touched his nose.

"A warning," he said. "She is expendable. And if Olivier complies, I'll let him live. He has been useful."

"And an old friend of yours."

Gable's mouth hung open, tongue red from the steak. "There are no friends in business."

"Of course," I said, staring at my shoes.

"We are all strangers to one another."

A stranger is about to have my baby, I wanted to say but wisely kept my fat mouth shut.

"You have been a revelation this year," he said, and I couldn't help but beam.

"This has been the best year of my life."

"I imagine so."

"Thank you for everything."

"Your dedication is thank you enough." He popped up on his heels scanning the room. "Marilyn and Peck haven't arrived yet?"

"No, I was looking for her too."

He wagged a finger. "I'm sure you have. She and I have our traditions too."

"A kiss at midnight?"

He tapped his nose. "If you don't mind?"

"Not at all."

"Maybe I can put the two of you on assignments together next year?"

"That would be great."

"Her and Peck deal with more complex scenarios. Would you be ready for more responsibility?"

"I'm ready for whatever you would ask of me."

He patted my head like a puppy. "I'm going to circle the room. Before midnight I will call a toast. Make sure everyone corrals in the main room."

"Certainly, Gable."

"The eighties are going to rock in a way you cannot even comprehend. Our new client..."

"The distributor?"

"He will take us to such great heights."

I sniffed, shifting around the coke attached to my nostrils.

"Don't sample the product too much." He lightly slapped my cheek. Before I could reply, he was already mingling, an exaggerated laugh erupting from his throat. A Doris Day and Rock Hudson joined in whatever joke had been told. The three cackling so loud it could break thin glass. A Lana Turner and Montgomery Clift found their way over. Then a Ginger Rodgers and Gene Kelly. Burt Lancaster and a William Powell. None of them operatives. Clients dressing up for the night. But still leaning toward their leader, the boss with the capital B, the one who could get whatever they desired, and therefore, laughing along with the only god they'd ever come close enough to touch.

31

"Knock on Wood" was playing when Marilyn entered the restaurant with peck.

She seemed anxious, rushing to get away from him. He took a quick step to go after her and then made his way to the bar instead. As she fled into the bathroom, I noticed she had a limp. I went right for him. A couple of drinks plus some blow had made me braver than usual. He was already sucking down a dark liquor when I reached the bar.

"Errol," he said, his voice reeking of smugness. He angled his body away from me, chatting with an Ingrid Bergman.

"What the fuck, man?" I said, knocking into his shoulder as Amii Stewart sang for all to "Knock on Wood".

He maneuvered as so not to spill his drink. Sucking on the back of his teeth, he turned around, met my eyes.

"Should I pretend that shove didn't happen?"

"What did you do to her?"

"To who?"

"To my girl."

The laughs began at the base of his throat, creeping out of his mouth. Peck had an uncanny ability to make your skin chill. Imaginary warning signs appearing around him.

"You have a girl?"

"Yeah. Marilyn. She came in with a limp."

"And you're assuming I'm the cause?"

"She didn't have a limp this morning."

He put his arm around me like a brother would, pulled me in close. Through his mouth hole, I could see twisted teeth and thin lips that were barely there.

"I don't think you realize the kind of work we do."

"Get the fuck offa me."

I whapped at his arm, got right in his face.

"If you ever touched her—"

"I did. I did touch her. Many, many times. She's smooth as cream."

"If you hurt her—".

"Hurt is not an easily definable word. What hurts one, may not affect another."

"If you ever make her feel bad..."

"You'll what?"

"I'll ice you."

He threw back his head, laughed at the heavens.

"Will you, little boy Flynn?"

"You'll never see it coming."

"You do and Gable will have you down at the bottom of the East River. Permanently. You'll join any others with cement blocks for shoes."

"I think you underestimate my relationship with Gable. I'm like a son."

"Did he say that?"

"He doesn't have to say it, I know."

"Well, you have it all figured out then, don't you? But what you haven't realized is my own relationship with Gable. The secrets I hold. That of his family."

My head felt battered around. "What? He has a family?"

"Of course he does. A lovely family. Wife, daughter and a baby. A white picket fence in the suburbs. He knows that if he ever turns on me, I'll tell every deranged criminal we associate with about his brood. They would be dead by the next morning."

I was stunned, unable to speak.

"The only power you can have with Gable is to have something on him. He might like you more than me, I'm sure he does, but that's meaningless, worthless. He only trades in the currency of fear. And I have him very afraid."

"What if he just iced you?"

"There are cassette tapes ready to be mailed out should I find a demise. So I get to do what I want, you-hear? And let me tell you, you green motherfucker, he appreciates my slyness. Because he would do exactly the same. We see each other. While you, Errol, are not enough of a surprise."

I decked him. I'd punched out people better, but made good contact with his left cheekbone. He was sturdy enough to barely move from the blow while my fist throbbed.

"I'll let you have that one for now," he said, touching the spot where I hit. He finished his drink and ordered another, dismissed me by pivoting in his stool. A few clients had noticed, whispered amongst them-selves. I worried that Gable had seen, but he wasn't around. Marilyn exited the bathroom, and I rushed over to her.

"Are you okay?" I asked.

She stared me down. "Hello to you too, Errol."

"You're limping." I pointed at her leg like she didn't understand.

"Casualty of the assignment. Turned an ankle."

"In your condition–"

I back-peddled, not meaning for it to come out like that.

"What about my condition?"

"Bette told me," I whispered into her ear, as if it should stay a secret. "When were you going to...?"

"That trifling bitch. And I wasn't hiding it from you. I was deciding what I wanted to do."

"Keep it. I want a child with you. I love you."

I almost felt myself getting down on one knee right there, but maintained my sanity.

"It's not so simple–"

"Why not?"

"Am I supposed to go assignments with a stroller?"

"We'll figure it out. Gable has a family."

She whipped her head closer. "How do you know that?"

"Peck. He said–"

"It's not his place to tell."

"I thought he had hurt you again. I went over to..."

"To what? Scare him? You don't have to save me, Errol."

"It's not okay for him to hurt you."

"He's untouchable, understand? He has a hold over Gable I'll never have."

"It's blackmail."

"It keeps him invincible. So when he needs to take out his aggression…"

"You're the target?"

"Whoever is close by."

"But you're with child now. You don't wanna put the baby in danger."

She caressed her stomach as if she'd already started creating a bond.

"I've always wanted a little girl," she said.

"Little Marilyn."

"She'd be more like Norma Jean likely, kinda luck I had."

"Two minutes till midnight," someone shouted from across the restaurant. The music lowered. Gable appeared from a dark corner, making his way over.

"You don't have to be everything that everyone else wants," I said to her, shocked at my honesty. The coke bringing it out.

Marilyn didn't respond. She curtsied at Gable. He led her away. With a minute left, their faces got close, intimate, like I was watching something I shouldn't be.

The countdown from ten began. At midnight they kissed, and she rested in his arms in such a way I wondered if he was the father of her child. I'd pegged Peck as a possibility but maybe she desired Gable most.

I had to get away. Rushing to the room where I took Bette before, I closed the door behind me. Breathed in until I stopped shaking. A woman lay across the couch, high heels kicked off and resting by its side.

"I'm sorry, I didn't notice you—"

I peered closer to discover Katherine Hepburn, her mouth hanging open. She could be sleeping but wasn't making a sound. I put my ear to her mouth and heard nothing. Spencer Tracy had already struck and she hadn't made into the new decade.

1980.

With all the death surrounding me, I wondered how much of it I'd get to see?

1980

32

I HADN'T SEEN MY FOLKS OR EMILE IN TOO LONG SO I went over to watch the steelers play the rams in the super bowl.

Pop was a diehard Giants fan, but after losing the season with a 4-12 record he was ready to be done with them.

"Fucking Phil Simms," was all he said when I walked in with a six pack. It had been months since we'd seen one another. I shouldn't have expected a better hello.

"Got any money on the game?" I asked, and he gave me a lingering look. Like *don't freakin' talk about money around your ma*.

Ma was feeding Emile potatoes cut up in tiny little bites. Most of the pieces spilled from his mouth and collected in a heap on the floor.

I handed Pop a brew and we clinked bottles. Heading over, I'd almost forgotten to take off my Errol Flynn mask. I tried to remember the last time I was naked without it.

"How's Marilyn doing?" Ma asked. She brushed her hair from her face, the roots going white. Looking at pictures of her family, they all had flowing stark-white hair.

"Oh, she's good, Ma. Workin' tonight."

Yesterday, Marilyn and I had an argument. I told her Gable said we could do missions together. When she didn't respond, I got pissed. I yelled that she should ask Gable to be my partner instead of Peck's. When she admitted she couldn't, I raised my voice until we were screaming over one another. "You like getting abused by him," I said, unable to see her response behind the mask. She grabbed her coat and left.

I spent too long waiting for her to return. I thought about contacting Maggs to grab some beers, but it had been forever since we hung out and I imagined it'd be awkward.

"She's very pretty," Ma said, and then nodded at my dad to respond until he agreed.

She planted a kiss on my cheek, but it felt distant, like it was her duty rather than out of love. She couldn't look me in the eye.

"Do you guys need money?" I asked, searching my pockets and coming up with a stack of bills.

"Oh, Jakey, no, it's all right."

The money was even harder for her to look at. She pushed my hand away.

"But I want to give you guys—"

"Your da's a good provider," she said. "We don't need more."

What she meant was, your money was too dirty for me to consider it real.

Emile made a noise, the sputtering sound of a motor

dying. Usually it meant he crapped his diapers. Ma went into martyr mode and wheeled him into the bathroom.

"I've been meaning to talk to you," Pop said, under his breath. He turned up the game, the Rams leading 13-10.

"What is it, Pop?"

"I'm gonna say as little as possible to protect ya."

"Pop, you can tell me–"

"Jake, don't argue. I'm sure you know Dick Mancini's dead."

Do I ever? I wanted to say.

"Anyway, his crew still runs the neighborhood, maybe not with as tight a fist as before but they have clout. They've been...lurking around."

"What for?"

He sipped his beer, scratched his stomach. "Seem to think I'm involved with his death somehow. Have a million questions."

"But why do they think you...?"

"Word is they've been harassing everyone. Trying to prove they can still pose fear. Mancini had a lot of enemies. Anyway, it's been worrying your ma. She's seen them outside, leaning against their car, eyes on our building."

"What do you want me to do?"

"The company you work for, right, they can make things happen?"

"Yeah, wishes, we grant wishes–"

"Just put the fear in them. So Ma won't worry so much. That good woman has enough on her plate."

"Have they threatened you?"

"Not in so much words."

The Steelers scored a touchdown and the fans went crazy.

"I'm about to turn this off," Pop said. "I don't care who wins if the Giants ain't there."

I wanted to have the Card help Pop, but I knew Gable would steer clear. Because I iced Mancini, Gable wouldn't take any chances getting it tied back the Card.

"I'll see what I can do," I said, and Pop drained the rest of his beer.

"Stacks of cash," he muttered. "I'm aware of who you are…"

"What was that?" I asked. When he didn't answer, I said, "I'm aware of who you are too."

"I was who I needed to be," Pop said.

"Same here."

"Are you?" He paid attention to the game, reached into a bowl of popcorn and pulled out a handful.

"I'm really good at what I'm doing, Pop."

"And what is it you exactly do?"

"I fulfill wishes."

"Ah, is that what they tell you?"

"No, it's just… I don't get you, Pop. First you ask me for a favor, then you insult me. If you're so disappointed in me…"

"Listen, and listen to me good, Jake. I got in over my head a long time ago. And when you do, you never get out of it. Let's not pretend between the two of us anymore. You're working for bad guys, and I was too. Because that kid in there didn't stand a chance unless we had funds. But you, no one's depending on you. You don't have to throw away your soul."

"This is why I don't come back here. And I do have people depending on me, you guys."

"We're fine without your cash."

"And what about your other wish?"

"That's different. And if you don't want to do anything to help, then don't."

"It ain't that, Pop. I just want you be proud of like one thing I've done in my life. I know you've bailed me outta jail too many times. I know I'll always make you worry."

"Your ma stays up all night sometime wondering where you are, the troubles you're getting in."

"I can take care of myself."

"I don't think you can. Because I thought I could too and I couldn't. If I didn't get lucky by Mancini getting his throat slit, I'd still owe him. And maybe that's why his crew still hangs around, because they're still looking to get paid."

"So what do you want? My company to get rid of them?"

We were yelling at each other over the sounds of the game.

"Quiet or your ma will hear."

"She already knows."

"It's different to hear from her own son's mouth he's a criminal."

"Fine, I'm a criminal, Pop. I've done real shitty things. But you need me right now."

"Okay, yeah, whatever." He was drunk and starting to slur. "You get these guys off my back, away from my family. But you have to understand what I'm asking you."

"I know, you want them removed."

He shook a finger back and forth, closed one eye and zeroed in on my soul. "Not just that,

Jakey, after you do this for us, I want you gone too."

It was like someone took an ice cream scooper and scooped out my heart, left it beating and bloody on the ground for the rats to chew up.

"What? You don't mean—"

"I do, Jakey. Because you'll bring destruction to us if you don't."

"And what's Ma say about this?"

"Ma was one who told me to tell you."

I knocked over a lamp because it was the closest thing in reach. It shattered, the bulb still lit before fizzing out.

"She's thinks it ain't safe with you around. So you do this for us, but if you stick with your employers, then we'll have to say goodbye."

"But I love you guys."

Pop rose from his chair, holding onto the armrest for support. In the bathroom, Emile was howling, as if he could feel my pain. Pop was breathing heavy. I thought he might be having a heart attack or something, but he was trying not to cry. It took everything in him to keep strong.

"I'm asking you, Jakey," he said, his hand on my shoulder. "You're gonna have to choose. But I fear you may not have a choice anymore."

"What do you mean?"

"Once you're in with those kinds of people, they don't let you leave so easily. Mancini was the same. Twenty years I did his bidding, wrestled with my conscience, lost myself. I hate that you've followed in my footsteps. I set a poor example."

I put my hand on his shoulder and we stood there, not hugging, but the closest we'd come in some time.

"You didn't, Pop."

"Go," he said. "Before your ma comes out of the bathroom. I don't want her to make a scene."

And so I left, even though it pained me to do so. To not get a last hug from my ma, or even try to initiate one with Pop. They were good parents, even though we'd been at odds for most of my upbringing. It was all me. I wasn't easy. Stubborn. Prone to troublemaking. Not satisfied when I was still, only in flight.

The snow licked at my face on the way back to Marilyn's, swirling around from the wind tunnel the streets created. I thought of continuing this life as an orphan. No ties holding me back. I could be whoever I wanted without fear of repercussions. Maybe they needed to let me go. Gable would be pleased with the news. To be my only father now. To have nothing in the way of sculpting me into his dream operative. Ending ties with my family the one thing that could truly move me up to station agent status.

33

I WENT TO SLEEP THAT NIGHT WAITING FOR Marilyn and feeling like I was entirely alone in this world. But she never returned and I was forced to make do with an old mask of hers that had been shoved in the back of a drawer. I placed it on the pillow beside me as if she was there. When I woke in the middle of the night to the sound of a large crash, I thought she had actually come alive.

Shaking away my half sleep, I threw off the covers and adjusted my eyes to the dark. The window had been broken and glass scattered across the floor. Trying not to step on it and cut my bare feet, I saw what looked like a bowling ball bag.

"What the fuck?"

Outside the snow still fell, whipping into the apartment through the giant hole in the window. My fingers shook as they went to unzip the bag. A tuft of hair poked out, the smell rancid. I opened the bag further to find a decapitated head. Stumbling back, I retched to the side, my puke smelling of too much beer. *This is a dream*, I told myself. The only possible solution. I squeezed my eyes shut to will myself to wake. But when I opened them, a head stared back at me. The head of my old friend Maggs.

The next few hours passed in a confused frenzy. Shock, awe, sadness, regret, anger, devastation. I wept with the bloody head in my lap. I called the Card but no one answered since it was the middle of the night. So I zipped up the head in the bag and made my way down to Georgie's place in Chinatown.

The subway empty at such an early time in the morning. Just me and the head in my lap and a scuzzed out homeless guy shouting for half dollars. I hadn't talked to Georgie since the incident with my Pop in the van, but I didn't know anyone else. This had to be Mancini's guys retaliating for either what they thought Pop did to their boss, or what they knew I'd done. I was glad the Card hadn't picked up the phone because this was not a mess they'd want to be mixed up with. In fact, it would greatly lessen my chances of becoming a station agent.

During the train ride, I mourned Maggs. I remembered the time in our school cafeteria when he drank too much milk and laughed so hard it spewed from his nostrils. Or when I dared him to eat his live goldfish, Kenny. Or when we'd steal newspapers from the stand and sell them for half the price a few blocks up during a sweltering summer when all we wanted was money to go to the movies that would be air conditioned. Or the time we shared a girlfriend and when she asked us to cross swords, we told her to take her hike. The time we hitched a ride to Philly just to get cheesesteaks. The year after the Son of Sam when we both dressed as him for Halloween. The way he'd laugh so hard and throw his head back, all teeth. His long locks of hair that always made me envious. The time he crooned Sinatra songs on a street corner and made almost fifty bucks. When we were kids and pricked our thumbs and swore we were blood brothers. In the train car, I lit the tip of a pen and drew the hot ballpoint across the inside of my wrist. I didn't kill Maggs directly, but I was responsible for his death. It would be a mark I'd bear for the rest of my worthless life.

When I reached Chinatown, I ran up the stairs to Georgie's place and pounded on the door. He opened it wearing pajamas like a little kid.

"Jake, what the hell?" he asked, squinting at the powerful light from the hallway.

"It's Maggs," I said, thrusting the bowling ball bag into his hands. "They killed him."

Georgie pulled me inside, set the bag on the table and slowly unzipped. I watched him go through the same stages I'd just went through hours ago. Once he calmed down, he swore revenge on whoever did this and we figured it had to be Mancini's guys. We rang up Jack with the Nose and headed to Hell's Kitchen.

Mancini had three guys on his payroll. A little person named Sam who shot his victims in the groin. A tall beanpole named Sandy who looked like a gust of wind would knock him over. And a fat man named Fat Charley. None of them had a family so we didn't have to worry about any collateral damage. No one was home at Sam's place or Sandy's, but sure enough, they all gathered for an all-night game of poker with three other degenerates from a different mob boss's crew.

Jack with the Nose knocked on the door, and when

someone asked who it was, we said we were late to the game. There was some grumbling from behind the door, but finally it opened and Jack with the Nose punched whoever was dumb enough to let us inside. The guys all went to reach for their pieces, but we were too fast. Jack with the Nose plugged the one who opened the door, a dummy from the other crew. That crew consisted of two inept underlings who fumbled with their guns before Georgie got them both —pow, pow.

Now only Mancini's guys remained. We had them place their guns on the table that Jack with the Nose collected. Then we took out Maggs's head and made it the centerpiece.

"What do you have to say for this?" I yelled. I'd become possessed, clearly having left my body, a creature running on pure sacrifice.

Mancini's crew blinked at one another in confusion.

"Are you trying to hurt my pop?" I thundered. "Who's after my pop?"

"We just..." Sandy began to say. "Wanted to scare him."

"Fuck you," I said, and shot him between the eyes.

Sam was shaking now, a terrified leaf. I stuck the gun in his cheek.

"You leave my pop alone."

He threw his hands in the air, his voice sounding like it was full of helium. "We will. We will!"

"You disgust me."

I went to pull the trigger, but Fat Charley cleared his throat.

"Jakey," he said, like we were buddies. We knew

each other in the neighborhood but had never spoken before. "You don't want to do this."

"Maggs was my best friend!"

"We didn't touch him." He indicated the cigarette pack stuffed in his front pocket. "Can I? Can I please? If my time is limited."

I nodded it was okay. He slid a cigarette out, threw it between his walrus lips, and puffed in delight.

"Decapitation?" he said. "We don't go that far. We were trying to figure out who did Mancini in. Knew your pop worked for us, just wanted to see what he knew."

"I killed Mancini. I killed him you motherfuckers."

Sam growled under his breath.

"But Maggs, we knew Maggs, we liked Maggs. Maggs was a good guy," Fat Charley said. "We wouldn't have done him like this. Not to get back at you."

"How am I supposed to believe that?"

Fat Charley shrugged his massive shoulders. "We can all walk away from this. We'll tell Abe's crew that we have no idea who hit the poker game. Look, take our winnings..." He shoved the cash on the table at Georgie. "Take it all. And Sam and I, we'll go far away. We've been looking for a clean break. Right, Sam?"

"He killed our boss," Sam peeped.

"Right, he did. But what are we gonna do about it?" Fat Charley paused to relish in a puff. "Have a vendetta forever? This is our chance out of the game. It's a sign from above."

He made a cross over his chest. "I truly believe this. That everything happens for a reason. Jakey. We did not kill your friend."

I eased the gun off of Sam. Locked eyes with Georgie and Jack with the Nose, who seemed to nod.

Just then, Sam bit down hard on my left hand. I tried shake him off but like a dog with his bone he wouldn't let go. Finally, I flung him so hard that he whapped against the wall, slid down in tears. He leaped for his gun but Georgie was quicker, punting him out of our way and firing into his chest. He clutched his guts spilling out, asking "why, why?"

"He is not me and I am not him," Fat Charley swore. His hands to the sky. "I could help you. I could find out who did this, but it was *not* me."

"I don't trust him," Jack with the Nose said, cocking his gun. Fat Charley whimpered.

"I'm gonna give you a week," I said, and Fat Charley seemed to deflate after holding his breath out of fear. "You find out who did this to Maggs, or you wind up in a bag too."

We left him to deal with the chaos. Georgie and Jack with the Nose asking me why I let him go, but Fat Charley wasn't my concern. He had no one left on his side, he'd do our bidding. Afterwards, we were hungry and Georgie and Jack with the Nose didn't know what would be open so I suggested the Waverly Diner where we could have omelets in a pan brought sizzling to our tableside.

34

WE LEFT THE BOWLING BALL BAG WITH MAGGS'
head by a police station and went our separate ways.

When I got home, Marilyn still wasn't there so I did
a few lines and watched the news. The Steelers had
come back and beat the Rams 31-19 in the Super Bowl.
Two hundred people were killed when the Corralejas
building collapsed in Sincelejo, Colombia. Marilyn
waltzed in after I'd filled an entire ashtray with cigarette
butts. She didn't say hello, just hung up her coat and sat
beside me on the couch. We watched the terrible news.

"I was there," she said.

"What? Where?"

She lit a cigarette and directed the smoke toward
the television. "Colombia."

"For our client?"

She touched her masked nose.

"Is it...?"

"Gable will tell you when he thinks you're ready."

"You were there with Peck?"

She nodded, sucked hard.

"Maggs is dead," I said. She tilted her head. "Decapitated. See that window?" I thrust a thumb back toward where I'd attempted to tape up the glass. "Someone threw his head right through."

"I'm sorry," she said. I could tell she was trying to be comforting. It was a concept she hadn't mastered. "Do you know who did it?"

I shook my head.

"Come here."

She directed me toward her bosom, lay my head down. Stroked the hair from my mask, not my own. Placed her chin on top of my head so I could hear her heart.

"I thought it might be Mancini's guys," I said. "They'd been bothering my pop. But I don't think so. Someone was sending a message."

"Looks like."

"What other enemies do we have?"

"This kind of business. Who knows? Come."

She led me to the bed where for a half an hour I was able to forget my concerns. After we were done, they came back full-throttle.

"My folks don't want me around anymore," I said, to the cracks in the ceiling.

"Family is not always a positive thing," she said. "Having no one worrying about you, it's freeing."

"I'd been thinking the same thing."

"I'm hungry."

She went to the kitchen, brought back a bologna sandwich that she ate as if it was the last sandwich in the world. She swept away the crumbs between us.

"I worry about you," I said, turning on my shoulder so we were nose-to-nose.

"Oh, Errol."

"That's why I want to work together so I don't have to think about all the terrible things that could be happening to you."

"Okay," she said, as swirls of bologna hung in the air.

"Really?"

"I'm growing tired of Peck," she said. "This trip solidified it."

"What did he do?"

"We stayed in adjoining hotel rooms in Medellin. With the cocaine business there, the city pulses. Anyway, we had brokered a hefty deal, that's all I can say about that for now. And so we went celebrating all night at a club. I crawled back to my room, got into bed, and heard violent cries coming from behind the wall. So I picked myself up and knocked on his door. No one answered. When I opened it, he was just torturing this poor young girl. She couldn't have been more than fourteen, fifteen tops. I smelled her blood when I walked in. It seemed like he'd tossed her against the wall, repeatedly, until her skull burst. She lay broken on the ground, a busted doll. He had a knife in his hands, dipped in red. His eyes spinning. When he gets like that, it's best to leave him alone so I ran out and he chased me down the hall. I was barefoot and running outside, the pavement cutting into my soles. Down the street with the knife held high, he followed. I thought I might die, nothing to defend myself. Finally, he tired out. Collapsed in the middle of the street, winded. I went back to the hotel room, packed a suitcase, and got the first plane out of there."

"Jesus, Marilyn, this is insane. And with you pregnant? Where is he?"

"I don't know. Probably back in Colombia."

"Does Gable know?"

She shrugged one shoulder.

"I realize Gable is afraid of Peck revealing his secrets, but this is ridiculous."

I was amped up. Bounced out of bed, threw on jeans, and a paisley shirt.

"What are you doing?" she asked.

"It's nearly morning, we're going down to the Card."

She watched me continue to dress, didn't budge.

"Marilyn!"

"I just want to sleep."

I tossed her a blouse and pants, got her heavy coat off the hook. She sat up and I dressed her, first the blouse then wiggled her legs into the pants. Once I had the coat on, we left and took a taxi down. Sure enough, Bette was there to greet us.

"He's in," Bette said, through her cigarette, typing away.

"Have you seen Peck?" I asked.

She stopped typing. "He's still out of the country on business."

"He nearly killed her," I said, pointing at Marilyn who shrunk in the corner. Bette stifled an emerging smile.

I grabbed Marilyn's hand and pulled her into Gable's office. We'd caught him off guard. He'd just finished a phone call and seemed rattled, only because he usually appeared so calm.

"Marilyn?" he asked, spooked to see her. "I didn't except you back."

"Everything went fine with the client," she said.

He exhaled. "Good, good."

"We're here because of Peck," I said, no time for bullshitting.

"Errol," Marilyn hissed, sinking her nails into my wrist.

"No, he has to know this," I said. "Peck killed a young girl and chased Marilyn down the street with a knife."

I was about to add that she was pregnant, but since Gable didn't know yet I kept silent.

"Marilyn, is this true?" Gable asked.

"You don't have to protect him," I whispered.

"He was unhinged," she managed to say. "The pressure of the mission. We were celebrating, letting off steam."

"That's not how you let off steam," I said.

"Errol, please," she said, quietly.

"Did he hurt you?" Gable asked, the tone of his voice more concerned than I'd heard it be before.

"No... Well, just scared me I guess."

"Okay," Gable replied. "I will have a talk with him when he gets back."

"Thank you, Gable."

He kissed her on the cheek and then they both turned to me satisfied.

"That's it?" I asked, flummoxed.

"Errol, I have to hear both sides," Gable said.

"He's been abusing her since I got here."

"Marilyn," Gable said, full of concern again. "If you would give us a second."

"Of course," she said, and left the room.

"It's never too early for brandy, is it?" Gable asked, pouring two glasses and handing me one. He clinked before I could refuse. "Errol, I'd ask you not to get involved."

"I can't sit back..."

"I said, do *not* get involved."

He raised his voice, a menacing thunder. I went to speak, then stopped myself.

"He's hurt her."

"I know," he said, regaining control over his emotions.

"I can't watch it happen."

"I've made Peck my station agent," Gable said. "It gives him more of a free reign."

"But..."

"He's an animal, you don't have to tell me that."

"Are you afraid of him revealing things about you?"

The room got still. The sound of the early morning city muted behind the window. Gable tapped his glass with his fingernails, each tap a sharp ping. I wanted to take it back, but it was too late. It would forever be out there.

"And what do you think he might have on me?"

"I'm sorry, I didn't mean... It was something he said."

Gable sucked at the back of his teeth. "Then say it."

"Your family."

He placed his drink down, stepped closer. I could smell the sugary liquor on his breath.

"And what did he precisely say?"

"That if anything happened to him, he would make sure your family was targeted."

Again, a silence: prickling, prodding. I had the sudden urge to piss violently. Then he let out a roaring laugh that must've reached the depths below.

"He was fucking with you, Errol."

"He said it was why you couldn't stop him from doing what he wanted."

Gable squeezed my shoulder, dug his fingers into a knot.

"I don't have a family, Errol."

"Oh."

"How could I possibly run this kind of business with responsibilities at home?"

"I wondered..."

"Peck likes to cause chaos, he feeds off on it. And he is my best operative, always has been. Never a wish he hasn't fulfilled."

"I'm just worried about Marilyn."

"Don't be. Marilyn will outlast the cockroaches after an apocalypse. She runs on pure fury."

"You had mentioned before about us working together?"

He nodded a few times as if he was letting it sink in.

"I want more responsibility," I said. "Give me a mission with her. If Peck is so good, he can work on his own. Let me prove to you—"

He held up his hand. "All right, Errol. All right. You've convinced me. I have something in mind. And maybe it would be best to keep Marilyn and Peck apart for the time being."

"Thank you. Thank you, sir. Truly."

"I'm glad this was brought to my attention," he said,

directing me toward the door. I felt unsettled, like he would explode with rage once I left: for questioning him, for speaking my mind.

"My friend Maggs is dead," I said, unsure why I'd felt the need to let him know at that exact moment.

He had his hand on the doorknob, let go.

"What happened?"

"Someone cut off of his head and tossed it through my window."

I heard him audibly swallow.

"And do you know who did this?"

"No," I said, trying not to cry but the tears were spilling. Luckily, the mask kept them hidden.

"Let the Card help you," he said. "He once was one of us and we don't take kindly to being fucked with." He turned the doorknob and opened the door. "Now I must make a call. If you would excuse me."

The door slammed behind me, causing me to jump a little.

"What did he say?" Marilyn asked, breathless.

"Looks like you have a new partner," I said.

Bette's typing slowed, her ear perked our way, listening close. The phone rang and she answered, talking softly.

"Oh, Errol," Marilyn said, but she wasn't elated, her tone disappointed as if I'd ruined her party. "Oh, Errol."

She shook her head over and over until tears loosened from her eye holes.

35

THE WESTCHESTER COUNTY AIRPORT WAS BUILT in 1942 as a home to an Air National Guard unit to protect New York City's water supply system.

For Marilyn and I, we were scheduled to meet our mystery client, or at least one of his underlings, during the middle of the night after the air traffic controllers were all paid off. We had an estimated arrival time and waited in White Plains blowing cold air into our gloved hands. After leaving the Card's offices, Marilyn slept through the day so we hadn't really discussed what had happened.

"Are you mad at me for telling Gable about Peck?" I asked, treading cautiously.

"Mad is not the right word. I'm apprehensive."

"Why?"

"You can't show weakness to Gable. He'll use it."

"Use it for what?"

"I've seen it before."

She seemed more melancholy than usual. She turned to the side and puked over her shoulder.

"Are you all right?"

"It's the baby, it's normal."

"Have you had a doctor check you out? I can go with you."

"Errol, I need you to understand that I haven't decided what I'm going to do."

I wanted to ask if it was definitely mine, but it wasn't the right time. I kissed her cheek.

"Whatever you choose I support."

"Thank you."

From out of the foggy sky, a propeller plane appeared, stirring up the dust. We shielded our eyes. The runway lit up and the plane landed. Marilyn and I rushed over. A rail-thin man with a mustache and concave belly exited the plane. He whipped off his goggles. Did Escobar know how to fly planes? I tried to match this man up with what I'd seen from Escobar over the news, but it was too dark out.

"Marilyn," he said to her, with a Spanish accent.

She didn't refer to him by name. He directed us around to the back of the plane that was piled high with suitcases. He and Marilyn were talking low while I hefted the suitcases onto the ground. I counted twelve.

"Open one," he said. "Make sure."

Inside of the first suitcase had to be about twenty bricks of cocaine, pure cut. I assumed straight from Colombia.

"Looks good?"

My gums watered. One by one I put them in the truck and backseat of the car. I watched Marilyn hand the man a purse filled with what was likely money. The man got back in the plane. The propeller started spinning and he was gone.

We brought the drugs back to our place. Opened each suitcase and stared in wonder at the sheer amount. The phone rang and it was Gable. Through the squawking from the receiver, I could hear he was pleased. He didn't want the drugs kept at the offices. He told her we would house it all. She hung up the phone and broke open a brick with her long fingernail, scooped some up, and sniffed.

"We need some kind of perk," she said.

I knew she shouldn't be snorting drugs with a baby, but I was too afraid to question. I wanted to enjoy our success. We were a team. We got blazingly high and found our way into each other arms, then went down to the Odeon for all-night oysters and cocktails.

"What can I get you, Miss Monroe?" the bartender asked, enamored.

"Two sloe gin fizzes for me and my guy."

My guy. I put my arm around her and drew her close. After two drinks in, she began to sway.

"I had the strangest dream the other day," she said. "I wasn't Marilyn. I was just me. It's rare for me to dream of her. I've heard that when you dream of someone you haven't thought of in a long time your brain is about to get rid of their memory and it's your subconscious' last-ditch effort to keep them alive. Anyway, I was waiting at the docks for a boat. I was nervous it wasn't coming. I was running from something. My stomach was large, and I felt my child kick. Every sound made me jump, worrying it was foretelling my demise. But the boat came and I got on and sailed away."

"Where did you go?"

"I don't think I knew, only that it was...away."

"That makes me sad."

"Why?"

"Because I wasn't there with you."

"No, you weren't. And I think, I knew you were dead, or about to be. And that if I would have stayed, I'd be dead too. When I was a child, I had psychic abilities, or rather, my dreams did. They spoke of visions. They saw my future. They predicted the Card long before I joined."

She sipped at her sloe gin.

"I have something to confess to you, Errol."

The Odeon was practically silent. We were the only patrons besides a janitor mopping up the floor and the bartender fiddling with the radio, the song "Boys Don't Cry" by the Cure playing.

"It's okay, you can tell me anything."

"Can I? You won't be angry with me?"

"Never."

"I'm not sure the baby is yours."

Her words swallowed up the atmosphere, made my skin prickle.

"Whose then?" I managed to say.

She shrugged her shoulders.

"Peck?"

She tilted her head from side to side.

"Gable?"

She froze, her tongue escaping through her mouth hole and licking her masked lips.

"Did they force you?"

"No, never."

I let the information sink in. "I don't care."

"Errol, you don't have to lie."

"No, I really don't care. I would raise it as my own. That would be enough."

"I have to tell Gable."

The back of my neck got hot. In no way would this turn out well. Either he'd be upset and insist on aborting the baby, or make sure he'd take care of raising it.

"Why? It's likely mine. You've been with me more, right?"

"Of course, Errol. It was just one time with each of them."

"Then pretend it never happened."

"I can't..."

"We're so good at pretending, you and I. Aren't we? We've become different people. We've hid ourselves well. Why can't you hide this?"

"You can't hide anything from him, don't you see? Likely, he already knows."

She finished her drink.

"We should go home."

We cabbed it back to our place, found solace in some sniffs of powder.

"I meant it," I said. "I don't care. Just think before you tell him."

"I will."

I stared at all the suitcases crowding the apartment.

"What does Gable expect us to do with all of this?"

"Sell it to the masses," she said, rubbing another pinch into her gums before she turned out the lamp and went to bed. "Every last drop."

36

THE NEXT MONTHS PASSED IN A BLUR OF attempting to move the coke.

One by one the suitcases left our apartment until none remained. We worked well as a team. Marilyn was so thin she was barely showing, and I had convinced her not to tell Gable. Peck also remained in Colombia to handle business over there so I didn't have to worry about him mucking things up. Maggs's murderer stayed a mystery. Fat Charley gave me updates at the beginning but then he vanished, either dead or he took off far away from the city.

In fact, everything was going great until I was in a bar one night listening to Gary Newman's "Cars" when someone placed a hand on my shoulder. I'd been trained to react with a chop to the neck and almost cut off the breath of Olivier, who had slumped onto the stool next to me, weeping into his Cape Codder.

"You look terrible," I said. He was wearing his mask of course but the mask looked worn, falling to pieces.

"I miss her terribly," he said, and when I was about to ask "who," he responded "Katherine."

I led him outside to get some air. It was springtime and the night cool.

"Where have you been?" I asked.

"Brussels. My home. It just isn't the same."

"I'm sorry," I said, but I couldn't feel bad. He was responsible for her icing. They should've never tried to undermine Gable.

"I've thought of nothing but revenge," he said, as if he was being watched.

"You need to be careful."

"Fuck being careful. Fuck it all."

He shook his fists at the sky in a dramatic way, then reached into his coat pocket and caressed the gun sticking out.

"I have half a mind to march down to the office and put a slug in his brain."

"Now what will that do?"

"Give me the peace I deserve."

"You'll just wind up dying too."

"There's no reason to live."

He took off so fast I needed a moment to realize he was gone. I chased after him, leaped and tackled him to the ground. I wrestled the gun out of his hand and emptied the cartridge.

"Why?" he yelled. "Why do you protect him?"

"I'm actually protecting you right now."

"I know Marilyn is pregnant. I can tell."

His mask seemed to smile as if it had one upped me.

"So what? What are you saying?"

"I'll tell Gable."

"Unless what, you let me let you kill him?"

He tapped his nose and I slugged him in the face.

"Your friend..." he said, wiping the blood from his gushing nose. "Maggs."

I grabbed him by the collar and shook him like a doll. "What about him?"

"He was the mole."

I snapped his head against the ground.

"For a few bucks, he spilled on Gable," he said. "And then Gable let him go. I think Gable knew."

"Who cut his head off?" I yelled, slapping his cheeks.

"If he was my mole, who do you think?"

I spit in his eye. "Fuck you. Why should I believe anything you say? Maybe you iced him so you can put it on Gable."

"I wasn't in the country. I can prove that to you. I have an alibi. Does he?"

"He wouldn't do that?"

"What do you base your conclusion on? He's ruthless. He would cut his own family's throat."

"He doesn't have a family."

"Errol, of course he does. I knew him before. He has a wife and two children."

"But he told me..."

"When will you realize that all he spews are lies?"

I sat back, my palms digging into the pavement full of spit gum and garbage. I envisioned Gable slicing Maggs's head off and launching it through my window. Wiping the blood from his hands as if it was nothing. Going to the Odeon for a martini afterwards and forgetting his devilish ways.

"Let's end him for once."

I thought of Jim Jones and his cult of people

drinking their Kool-Aid and sacrificing their lives. Had I been as stupid? It was hard to admit, easier to deny. Gable was like a father, and a father wouldn't do something so cruel. Olivier was a jealous partner, capable of making up anything to further his cause.

"I'm going to tell him what you said," I replied. "He spared you after Katherine died, despite your duplicity. You should owe him."

"He'll have a gun to the back of your head if he thinks you've lied too," Olivier warned. "What if I told him you knew Maggs was the mole? How do you think he'd—"

I shut him up by knocking him out cold. One great punch that sent a tooth flying from his mouth. I left him on the street to get mugged. I told myself I didn't believe him. Deep down I did. But it was tucked so far in a corner I couldn't locate the truth. And I didn't want to so I left it there to nag at me when it would already be too late, my reckoning coming so swiftly and surely.

Had I known, I could've started counting the days.

37

I stormed into the Card's office, no clue what was I going to say to Gable.

He needed to know Olivier's threats, but also his accusations. If I was going to continue here, I had to trust Gable, not freak out that he could turn on me at any moment. Bette was at her desk, and I didn't even let her open her mouth before I rushed inside. Gable was doing a line over a stack of papers. He snorted it up, poked and prodded at his fake nose.

"I wasn't expecting you," he said, straightening his tie.

"Olivier's in town. I stopped him from coming down here and putting a bullet in your head."

"I suppose you want a thank you?"

"I'd like to know the entire truth."

He rose from behind his desk and leaned against it, crossing his arms.

"I'm assuming Olivier has told you tall tales."

"Yeah, that you killed Maggs."

He laughed so softy I could barely hear.

"That's rich."

"Did you know he was the mole?"

"I do now, Errol."

"Who else would have iced him if it wasn't you or Mancini's crew?"

"Olivier..."

"He was out of the country."

"He could've had someone do it."

"Marilyn's pregnant."

"Ah," he said, pointing. "There's the truth you've been looking for."

"How long have you known?"

"Since I filled her up with my seed," he said, and when I stood there agog, he laughed louder this time. "I'm kidding, Errol."

"She told me the two of you..."

"I had a vasectomy. It would be impossible."

"After you had your two children?" I asked, with a wink.

"Okay, you got me. One untruth. I have a family. I don't like it known. There are few things dear to me and my family is a part of that small list." I went to speak, but he continued. "And yes, Peck knows about them and holds the threat over my head. But I applaud him for that. To know secrets is to have power. But he is unfortunately mistaken. The family he thinks I have belongs to someone else. I supplied him false details because I knew he might turn them against me one day."

"Is everything a lie?"

"Errol, don't look so forlorn. We all keep things

from one another. You kept Marilyn's condition from me, and I don't blame you."

"She still has time to decide if she'll keep it."

"I'm not here to make her decision, but in our line of work, it's a liability. I've had to be very careful in keeping my real family in the dark of what I do. The kids are young so that's simple, and my wife...well, she is very good at denial. That's why I chose her."

"But doesn't it bother you that Peck is planning to cut you down?"

"I'd question his sanity if he wasn't. Olivier too. These men are my best employees because they crave personal acceleration. It keeps them alert, focused. Are you telling me you've never questioned icing me?"

"No, man. I'm loyal."

"Oftentimes, the ones who proclaim they are loyal are the farthest from being so."

"Well, I'm true. I've given up everything for the Card, my family..."

"Yes, I am aware of that. And I do appreciate."

"What about Olivier? I knocked him out but that doesn't mean he still won't come after you."

"He is all bark. Ultimately, he needs me, and our rivalry. It's what keeps him sharp."

The intercom buzzed. "Gable, you have a call on line one," Bette said.

He held up his finger, answered the phone.

"Yes? Yes, Peck. Yes, good to hear. I think it is time for you to return home. We've unloaded the entire shipment. Yes, he is pleased. Take the red-eye and we'll brief in the morning."

He hung up the receiver.

"Peck is coming back?" I asked.

"Like I said in regards to Olivier and I, a little rivalry is good."

When I walked out of the door, Bette stopped typing.

"I suppose you know," she said. "That Peck's returning?"

"I heard."

"Looks like he'll be back working with Marilyn."

"How do you know that?"

She took out a nail file and scraped it across her fingers.

"Your mission is over. Onto the next."

"So? She and I can do it together."

She gestured for me to come closer. "The Boss ain't so pleased with the two of ya."

"How the fuck do you know that?"

"Language!"

"We unloaded the entire shipment together. That's a big deal."

"It was a guarantee the shipment would be sold off. He was seeing how you worked side by side and he don't like it. The closeness. He thought it would drive you apart."

"Why would he want to do that?"

She bobbed her hair. "Cause they're meant for each other, dummy."

"I don't think she feels the same."

"Don't matter. He's the Boss."

"You're fucking with me."

"Nuh-uh, I'm enlightening you. And it's likely his baby too."

"Were you listening at the door?"

"Of course I was! I need to type it all up." She shooed me away. "Now if you would excuse me."

She started typing. I tried to speak but she was slamming the keys, dwarfing my own fury. I left before I did anything foolish I might regret.

38

My sleep was interrupted by the sound of someone picking the lock of our front door.

I nudged Marilyn who rolled over on her face in response.

"Someone's trying to break in."

"Whattaretheygonnatake?" she mumbled, into her pillow.

I gave her a harder nudge. "Wake up."

Gable had given me a gun which I kept in the back of the sock drawer. I went to get it and saw it didn't have any bullets.

"Shit."

The door swung open, a figure lit from the outside hallway. I charged at the figure, knocking them down as we rolled around on the floor.

The lights cut on, Marilyn in her nightgown by the light switch. I was grappling at the face of our intruder, not a real face but a mask.

"Peck," Marilyn shrieked, as he punched me in the face and I staggered off of him.

Peck jumped to his feet, a swirl of untapped energy that had to be drug induced. He shifted from side to side ready to pounce.

"What the fuck are you doing?" I yelled, using my tee shirt to mop up the blood spewing from my nose.

"This cohabitating bullshit," he said. "While I slaved away in Colombia and you two bumped uglies."

"We've been living together for over a year," Marilyn said.

"Shut your hot mouth." He whipped out a gun and stuck it in my face. "Because of you I was landlocked in South America. Getting fucking dengue fever, vomiting my guts out."

"You seem fine," Marilyn said, with a yawn.

"Gable said I needed some space from you," Peck continued. "That our love triangle was causing issues. But did he send his newbie down to hell? No, I was shipped. There's a war going there right now. He stuck me right in the middle."

"Weren't you the one who could get him to do your bidding?" I asked, as he shoved the gun far enough into my cheek that I felt it against my tongue.

"Did she tell you?" Peck asked, his eyes inhuman. "She's pregnant and it's mine."

"How do you know that?"

"I doubt your virile enough."

"Peck, it's the middle of the night," Marilyn said, like she just realized. "We have work tomorrow. This is all exhausting."

"She's been playing us, buddy," Peck said. "Told you she loved you, right? I got the same bullshit. And I fell for it."

"I thought you were with Bette," I said.

"She doesn't move me like Marilyn."

"Then why'd you come after her with a knife?" I asked.

"We show our love in different ways. And let me tell you, buddy, she's stifled by you. Being Suzy Homemaker bores her. You bore her."

"And you scare her."

"At least I keep her feeling alive. You don't know what she's been through, what I've been through. We're two broken souls. We never stood a chance. I had cigarettes put out on me on the regular every time I questioned my dad. My first memory was his fist. And her, living on the streets before she was a teenager. Gable collected us wounded birds. Gave us a chance. You've always had a warm bed. You could never understand."

"So what? You're gonna kill me?"

"I want you to disappear. Tonight. Go far away and leave the Card alone. Because it's all turned to shit since you've arrived."

"I think you know I can't do that."

"I'll pull this trigger, I swear. Your brains will paint the carpet. And she'll cry but get over you. I'm the best thing for her."

"Peck, put down the gun," Marilyn said, in her baby voice. She shimmied over. "Lemme get you a drink, lemme calm you down."

"Tell me you'll be with me," he thundered.

"Of course, baby. You know you're my true love."

"Then tell him," Peck said. "How he means nothing to you."

She looked straight at me, sliced my heart in two. "You mean nothing to me, Errol. Peck's always been my guy. Like he said, we understand each other."

"You're lying," I said.

Peck knocked me in the forehead with the gun, a line of blood dripping between my eyes.

"She's not. I'm back. And you're dead."

"Lemme get you a drink, Peck," she said, pouting. "You must be so thirsty. Just a drink to sate your nerves. A bourbon. I could make you a bourbon."

"Yeah, all right, get me a bourbon."

"It'll make you feel better, love."

She disappeared into the kitchen. I heard the sound of ice being crushed and clinking in a glass. She shimmied back out.

"Here you go, love," I heard her say. She was standing behind him, her hand held high, an object clenched in her fist. She brought it down into his head. He let out a groan, an ice pick sticking up from his skull like an antenna.

"What just happened?" he asked, turning around.

"What I should have done a long time ago."

"My head hurts," he said.

"Not for long."

She wrenched the ice peck out of his skull and he collapsed to the floor, dead on impact.

"What did you do?" I asked, my teeth chattering.

"He was gonna kill ya," Marilyn said, wiping off the ice pick with a handkerchief.

As he lay on the floor, Peck looked as if he was sleeping, the mask not revealing his demise. I crouched down and tried to yank it off. It had stuck to his face and needed to be pulled with force. Once it snapped off, it shriveled up in my hand like it was ashamed for being removed.

I studied his actual face: gaping mouth and a fat

lolling tongue, bushy eyebrows and a beaked nose, completely bald. Older than I imagined. More like a mild-mannered accountant than a psychopath.

"I didn't mean anything I'd said," Marilyn cooed.

"Obviously."

"What are we gonna tell Gable?"

"That he was trying to kill me."

Marilyn shook her head. "It's not enough. He'll retaliate. They had a weird bond. Like Peck could do no wrong."

"Then we leave the body somewhere and let Gable find out for himself."

She shook head more ominously.

"He'll find out, then kill us both if we lied."

"How will he find out?"

"Errol, he knows everything. Somehow, I bet he's even aware Peck is over here right now."

The phone rang, a cry in the night. I nearly upchucked my heart. I let it ring: once, twice.

"Answer it!" Marilyn cried.

"Hello?" I said into the receiver, shivering.

"Put Peck on," Gable said.

I swallowed hard. "He...uh...stepped out."

"He just got there," Gable said. "Called me from the pay phone outside."

Fuck.

"Yeah, he wanted...uh...cigarettes. We didn't have none."

"Have him ring me when he gets back," Gable said, and hung up. I tossed the receiver of the phone as if it was made of scorpions, the busy signal pulsing, pulsing.

"What the fuck do we do?" I asked.

Marilyn coolly hung up the phone. "I'll have to tell him the truth."

"What will he do to you?"

She shrugged her shoulders. "Beats me, but what else can we do?"

"We can get outta here." I grabbed one of the suitcases that held the bricks of coke we sold. "Throw everything of yours in here and we'll leave."

"With what money?"

"I got some."

"Yeah, like a thousand bucks, that'll really get us far."

"We'll figure it out. Get jobs somewhere, raise this kid."

"This kid," she said, in a funny voice. "This kid, this kid. It's all anyone seems to talk about anymore."

"Marilyn, you're gonna be a mother."

"I could be dead by morning."

"Okay, okay, then we'll switch it around. Peck came after you, he was babbling nonsense. I already told Gable he chased you with a knife in Medellin. He was on drugs, came here jealous of us, and tried to kill you so I stabbed him with the ice pick."

She inspected the chipped nail polish on one nail. "I dunno."

"And you'll go away. And when it's safe I'll meet you. How about that?"

"It ain't gonna work, Errol."

"Fine, you'll just go away."

"He'll know if I get on a plane. He knows people at the airport."

"Then a boat. I'll get you on a boat."

I started throwing things in her suitcase.

"Stop, what makes you think I wanna leave?"

"So you'd rather die?"

"All right," she said, taking a deep breath. "You go to the Card, tell Gable, call me back here and we'll see what to do next. There's no use reacting until we know his reaction."

"I'd feel safer if you just went away."

"Ssshhh," she said, her finger over my lip. "Okay, then let's do this. I'll be waiting downstairs. If I don't hear from you after some time, I'll leave. I'll get on a boat. But I won't tell you where I've gone. Because if you know, he knows. Understand?"

"Bette told me he loved you, that he's obsessed with you. That he thinks it's his baby."

"He is. But obsessions aren't good. If he thinks he can't have me, he won't want anyone to."

"I have a real bad feeling, Marilyn. Like my stomach, it's all shook up."

"Baby," she said, kissing my face. "You go and tell him the story. Peck wanted to kill me and you killed him. If Gable gets angry, we're okay, it'll pass. If he's cordial, too nice about it all, that means we're fucked."

"Okay, I love you, Marilyn. I really do. I can't imagine life—"

"Let's go, let's get this over with," she said. "And I love you too. I realize I'd never known what kindness was till I met you."

I kissed her long and slow.

Since it might be our last one, I wanted to take my time.

39

BETTE OBSERVED ME LIKE SHE KNEW WHAT
Marilyn and I had done to peck.

I'd left Marilyn downstairs, warned her to hide in
the shadows. She would give me an hour and if I didn't
show, she'd get on a ferry that would take her up the
Hudson. From there, she could make her way to
Canada where she'd settle and wait for me. Stanstead,
Quebec bordered with Derby Line, Vermont. She had
an old friend who didn't live there anymore but fled
there when she had to get out of the States. She'd wait
for a week and then head to Saskatchewan where she
could properly get lost.

There was nothing keeping me here. The Card a
hoax. I only brought danger to my family the longer I
stayed. I'd cut all ties except for Marilyn and begin
anew. The thought exciting. I'd no longer be Jake
Barnum, or Errol Flynn. Her friend had a guy who
made IDs, and I could be whoever I wanted.

But first, I had to make it past Gable alive. If
Marilyn and I both ran, he'd surely come after us. He

had to be handled with finesse. Make him be the one to let us go. That would be the only way to survive.

But Bette's gaze already had me questioning our decisions.

"Where's Peck?" she asked, right away without even a hello.

"I don't know..."

"He went to your place even before he came to see me."

"Yeah, he needed..."

"Cigarettes. I know. Gable said. But he hardly smokes. I'm the one..."

"He went to get them for you."

She was typing throughout our conversation but stopped. I took the pause as a chance to walk past her into Gable's office.

Gable was talking to a man I sort of recognized. The man had John Lennon sunglasses and long hair he tucked behind his ears.

"Errol, this is Javier, you've met before," Gable said.

When he shook my hand, I remembered him as the pilot who delivered the suitcases of cocaine.

"Javier is taking over for Peck down in Colombia," Gable continued. "Running the show, not just transporting the product. He and I met a few years back down in a club in Miami. We both drove the same white Ferrari Berlinetta Boxers."

"Far out," I said.

"Are Marilyn and Peck here?" Javier asked. "I wanted to say hi."

He had a slithery quality, the ability to slip through small spaces because he was so thin. I needed him out of the room.

"Marilyn is waiting downstairs," I said, just to get him to go.

"Gable," Javier said, extending his hand. "I imagine this is the start of brand new territories for the both of us."

"Cheers to that."

They both tapped their noses and Javier left.

"Did Peck return?" Gable asked.

"That's what I need to talk to you about. Maybe you should sit down."

"I don't like the sound of that."

"This will be hard to hear."

"All right." He went around behind his desk and sat. "Hit me with your worst."

"Peck is dead."

He cracked his neck. "Come again?"

"He came to our place high on something and waving a gun around. I was afraid for Marilyn. So I stabbed him with an ice pick."

I winced as I expected a flood of rage, but Gable calmly rose and poured himself a drink. I noticed he didn't offer me one.

"Where is he now?"

"Peck? He's still at our place..."

He held up a finger and pushed the intercom button. "Bette, can you connect me with Spencer Tracy?"

"Sure thing," she said.

"Yes, Boss?" Spencer Tracy replied after a few rings.

"I'm going to need you to go over to Marilyn's place and clean up a mess. Chop suey and toss the parts in the Hudson."

"Aye aye."

Gable went back to his drink, took a cold sip that chilled my bones. "Now that he's taken care of–"

"I didn't have a choice, he was going to kill her," I continued, grasping at reality. Gable appeared far away as if I was looking at him through the wrong side of a pair of binoculars.

"Yes, I understand."

"Do you?"

"Simmer down, Errol. It's all right, everything is going to be all right."

His soothing tone unnerved me. I scanned for a weapon on him, but he held nothing except his drink.

"I was afraid I'd disappointed you, but I swear Marilyn would be dead if I didn't kill Peck first. He was obsessed."

Gable's eyes widened, as if I'd hit a trigger.

"Tell me how," he said.

"He insisted it was his baby, and...and he was angry at you for shipping him to Colombia. He brought up your family again."

The last part was a lie, but I figured it couldn't hurt to add.

"He said that with Marilyn and I out of the way, he'd be more respected at the Card. You'd realize his value. He was gonna come after you too, and I couldn't have that."

"Sssssh," Gable said, his hand on shoulder kneading a knot. "Where is Marilyn now?"

"I-I don't know."

"You said she was downstairs."

"I just needed that other man to leave the room so I could tell you what happened."

"So, she's not downstairs?"

He leaned at an angle so he could see out of the window. I did as well. Being on the second story, I could make out a blinding white dress and blonde hair against the dark morning. Gable turned back to me with a sigh.

"Were you afraid of my reaction?"

I shivered, the room ice cold. With chattering teeth, I murmured, "Yes."

"What did you think I was going to do? With Peck gone, my numbers have dwindled. I need you and Marilyn."

"Do you?"

"Yes, Errol." He pressed the intercom button. "Bette, Marilyn is downstairs. Please bring her up here."

"I can go..." I began to say.

"No need, Bette will."

"All right," Bette buzzed back.

He licked the top layer of his teeth. Something didn't feel right. I wondered if somehow, he'd given Bette a code to ice Marilyn. I was such an idiot for not lying that she was far from here.

"Peck was troubled," Gable finally said, because the silence had gotten uncomfortable. "He was my first hire, you know? Older than me but barely developed, still a child somewhat. Dragged through the foster system after being yanked out of an abusive home. The foster families might've even been worse, usually how it is. I like my operatives to be damaged. For this kind of work, you have to have been through a lot to understand what we do. It becomes a rehabilitation program of sorts. For example, you, *Errol*, are a different person than when you first arrived. Surer of yourself, tougher, stronger, more equipped to handle what's thrown at you. And I got you there."

He nodded until I finally agreed with him.

"I owe you a lot, Boss," I said, because I really meant it. I'd be in prison if the Card hadn't come along, probably still getting played by my old girlfriend Cheryl, uncertain that I'd have any kind of future that made me happy. And I had been happy since I found the Card. Through its high and lows, its death and destruction, it gave me purpose, meaning.

We heard the sound of a gun go off and my heart nearly shattered. Out the window, I saw a figure in a white dress running away, her brilliant platinum blonde hair reflecting in the sunrise.

Gable reached one hand into a side pocket that held a bulge. A gun? I couldn't stay to find out.

"Don't..." he began to say, but I was gone before he could finish his sentence, flying out of the office and down a flight of stairs, bursting outside and nearly tripping over a dead Bette Davis blocking the entrance, a bullet hole between her eyes.

"Fuck," I yelled crying. I scanned the block for Javier. At such an early hour, the street was empty. No sign of Marilyn either. She had vanished like I begged her to do. The sound of heavy footsteps on the stairs inside the building caused me to run faster than I ever had toward where I saw Marilyn flee, into the rising sun, the brilliant heat.

40

THE FERRY LEFT IN TWO HOURS SO I CABBED IT over to my folks place to say goodbye before I'd meet Marilyn at the dock.

Had no idea what I was going to say to them. There was a chance we'd never see each other again. Pop would be gruff about it, Emile clueless, but Ma would fall apart. When I got there, they all were at the dining table eating breakfast, Ma serving eggs.

"Jakey, what are ya doing...?"

"I don't have much time," I said, already breaking down. Tears and snot, a liquid mess. "I'm sorry, I'm so fucking sorry."

"Jakey, what's going on?" Ma asked.

Pop got up and slammed his chair into the table. "I thought I told ya not to come back here."

His face had turned an unnerving red, a vein in his neck pumping. Rage in his eyes behind coke-bottle glasses.

"Listen, just listen," I began, but Emile started wailing. When the kid wailed, he could wake people up blocks away. "Hey, hey, Emile," I said, sitting close to him. He had spit up the eggy mush Ma had made him. I grabbed a napkin and wiped it from his chin. "Don't cry, it's your older brother, Jakey."

His mouth opened to a big O trying to form my name.

"Hey, hey, I'm here. It's okay, little buddy."

I put my arm around his shoulder, held him close. He wiped his nose on my sleeve. It was too much. I was blubbering and needed to say my piece and get out of there.

"I gotta go away for some time." I was telling this to Emile, but my folks were the audience. Ma gasped, Pop wiped his glasses.

"Things are, they're not good," I continued.

"These people you got yourself involved with," Pop said, distributing his weight onto his good leg. "And for what? To be all cool."

"Pop, that ain't the reason."

"Then what? What was worth giving up your family?"

"I fell in love."

Sure, the Card had its appeal. The parties. The power they spoke about. But it all was about Marilyn. Take her out of the equation and I didn't need them. Everything I'd done there had been for her.

"That Marilyn Monroe looking floosy," Pop said. I could've hit him. If it'd been anyone else I would've socked them good.

"She's not a floosy, Pop."

"A temptress."

"I'd been to jail about five times for stupid shit. I was nothing special. She didn't tempt no one."

"You're good," Ma said, coming over and stroking my hair. "You're good."

"I'm not, Ma. I'm lousy."

"But we raised you to be good."

"This neighborhood, fucking Hell's Kitchen, exactly like it sounds," I said. "What happens to most guys my age from around here? We wind up in prison or dead. Those are the options. Well, I'm not doing neither. I'm getting away from the Card, from the Boss. I ain't doing their bidding anymore. I'm leaving with Marilyn. Because Pop's right. It ain't safe for you guys if I'm here."

Emile started wailing again. Ma ran over and cooed to calm him down.

"I won't hear of this, Jakey," she said. "We are a family, and we stick together."

"You don't know me," I said. "This..." I went to rip the mask off, not realizing that I hadn't kept it on. I'd ripped it off and left it in a garbage can when I ran from the Card's office.

"Whattaya mean I don't know you? I know my son."

"No, Ma, I'm rotten. Done rotten things. I've killed people."

She plugged her ears. I went over and wrenched her hands off of her head so she could hear.

"Listen, hell is waiting for me. I deserve it. But I'm not bringing you all down with me."

"Get out," Pop said, softly.

"Pop, lemme finish."

"Get the hell outta here, you louse," he yelled, louder than I ever heard him speak before.

"I love you all," I said, snot still streaming down my

face. "But I love her too. She's the only happiness I've ever really known. Lemme have that. I stay here and the Card will ice me. They'll ice you too, I wouldn't put it past them."

Ma shook her head back and forth. "No, I won't lose my son."

"Ma, listen to me." She kept shaking her head. "Ma!" I grabbed her by the shoulders, looked deep into her sad eyes. "Let me go."

"Jakey, I can't."

"But you have to. Ya have to." I let her go and Pop came to collect her.

"Saoirse, give us a minute. Take Emile into the other room."

She stared back like a ghost, between worlds, confused as to which way to go. Finally, she snapped into action: what she knew—Emile. The child she'd been put on Earth to take care of. I was a distraction. An abomination. She'd be better off without me.

She grabbed the handles of his wheelchair and led him away. She didn't look back because she'd melt if she did. She understood as much as she could handle. Her long red hair flowing down her back. Her nightgown wrapped around her pale body. An Irish song humming from her lips. She didn't deserve to be shackled to this family. She should have been a queen. But God didn't have that for her in his plan. It was why I found it tough to believe in Him because He never seemed to want the best for us. I'd go to church as a little kid, was even an Alter boy, gave up chocolate for lent. All for what? No one was looking out for you from above or anywhere else. I thought of something Ma told me once when I got into trouble for bullying a kid in class. She told me that St. Augustine said, "Right is right even if no one's doing it; wrong is wrong even if everyone's doing it." I'd followed the crowd and it led me to the principal's office. I hadn't learned a thing fifteen years later. I burned to give her one last hug, but that wouldn't be fair to her. She had already said goodbye, and I had to respect her wish.

I made for the door, but Pop grabbed my arm. Tears leaked from the corners of his eyes. He stammered, went to talk, and then stopped.

"I hate what I've put you through," I said.

"I know, son."

"I'm right to say I'm rotten."

"You're not. You're misguided and I'm partially to blame."

"No, Pop, you were..."

"Not around. Working. It's true that kids from this neighborhood only have a few options. We let each other down."

"Yes, we did."

He pulled me in for a bear hug. I didn't want to let go. Stay in his arms forever protected like when I was scared little kid who had a nightmare. He gripped me tight and then pushed me away. Turned his head so he didn't have to see me anymore. I slouched to the door, opened it for the very last time. Found myself under the dim light of a bulb that was about to pop. I could hear it crackling. An ending arriving.

It popped and chilled my bones. Gooseflesh along my arms. Shivering like I'd be drowning. By the time I got outside, I already missed them terribly. But they were my past. Marilyn would be the future for however longer I had on this rock.

So I ran west to the ferry to leave with my love. My feet taking flight. Soaring through the dirty streets, the garbage strewn, a city in decay. The pimps and whores along 42nd Street, the peep shows and ten-dollar nudie films where guys sat in the back and jerked off, the needles in the park, fresh and bloody, empty baggies of heroin and junkies with just white in their eyes, track-marks like birthmarks, exhaust from buses and cabs, smoke from cigarettes, gridlock and horns, shouting and brawls, dog shit and old gum that had turned black, this foul land I called home. That raised me and left me to dry. I'd watch it ebb away from a ferry boat with Marilyn in my arms, my nose at the back of her neck, taking a whiff of her acrylic fake hair. I'd leave her mask to float in the ocean, kiss her sliced cheeks, tell her how much I loved her and how special she was. We'd be giving up our lives for one another.

That was something, right?

Right?

41

I GOT TO THE DOCKS HALF AN HOUR BEFORE THE ferry was supposed to take off.

I scanned the area for Marilyn but couldn't find her anywhere. The boat hadn't pulled in yet so there wasn't a chance she had gotten on and I missed her. I buttoned up my coat because I was getting cold or maybe I was just shaky because I was nervous she wouldn't show. That Gable or another operative had found and prevented her from coming. She could be in danger or even dead as I waited.

The boat arrived and I watched the passengers get on one by one. They shouted for last call. My feet went to get on but my brain kept me from moving. The boat sailed away. The last ferry leaving at dusk.

I ran through my options. Hang around until the next boat hoping she was just running late. Go over to the Card's offices and try to rescue her if she was held captive. I had no gun on me and would surely be walking into my doom. The only friends I had left were Georgie and Jack with the Nose. I could head down to

Chinatown and hope to get them on my side to take down Gable. I lingered for a few minutes more and then shot over to Pell Street in a cab.

At their place, I buzzed up and Georgie answered.

"Yeah, who's this?"

"Jake, man, it's Jake. I'm in a bind. Can I come up?"

He didn't buzz me in right away. I thought I heard him conferring to someone, likely Jack with the Nose. Finally, the sound of a buzz warmed my heart and I burst inside, flew up the flight of stairs, and knocked on the door.

Jack with the Nose opened, his face scrunched in confusion.

"Thank you," I said, pushing past him. Georgie was at the table running bills through a counting machine. The air smelled of incense.

"I'm sorry to bother you," I said, pacing and pulling out hair. "Gable, he's after me. I killed Peck, actually Marilyn killed Peck and he ain't pleased. We're trying to get away, me and her, leave this life, this city, had it all planned out. She was supposed to meet me at the ferry docks but never showed. I think he has her."

Georgie and Jack with the Nose blinked in response.

"I need help, like I don't got no one else. Go down there with me to rescue her!"

"What's in it for us?" Jack with the Nose said, scratching his bulbous nose.

Georgie snapped his fingers in agreement.

"I'll...uh...owe you, for life. Anything you guys need."

"But you said you're leaving?" Georgie said, running a fresh stack of bills through the machine.

"Money?" I said. "We can get you. Send it securely once she and I are settled. Name your price."

The sound of a toilet flushing came from the bathroom off to the side. Georgie eyed Jack with the Nose, then both shot me a glance. My bowels clenched, a wave of nausea spreading.

"Who's there?" I asked.

Georgie responded with a slow shrug. The bathroom door swung open and I had to squint to see who it was in the low light of Georgie's tiny apartment. The sound of a gun cocked and Javier stood there pointing a pistol directly at me.

Georgie fed another stack of bills through the machine.

"Looks like someone got to us first with a better offer." Georgie nodded toward his fresh stack of bills.

Javier stalked into the front room. He was so lean it seemed that his skin was just draped over his bones. He swung the gun around and fixed his John Lennon sunglasses that had become askew.

"The Boss anticipated you might come here since your options are limited," Javier said.

"Don't take it personal, Jake," Georgie said. "It's not like we were ever close."

I backed up toward their nook of a kitchen. On the wall hung an array of cookery: pots and pans and a spatula. Javier kept pursuing, cornering me so I'd have no escape.

"Where's Marilyn?" I asked. "If you fuckers took her."

"You had it good, my friend," Javier said. "Gable spoke very highly of you. This could've ended very differently."

"Where is she?" I yelled.

Javier put a finger to his lips. "You wouldn't want the cops to be called, would you?"

"Where is she?" I asked, barely able to eke out the words, afraid of the answer.

"Wouldn't it ruin all the fun if you knew?" Javier asked.

Georgie fed another stack of bills through the machine.

"So what, you'll shoot me?" I asked Javier. "Just do it. End me. Fucking end me, I don't care anymore. If she's gone..."

"Who said she was gone?" Javier asked.

"Doesn't Gable have more important things to deal with than me? His client is Pablo Escobar, isn't it? We'll just disappear, Marilyn and I, we'll never make a peep again. He'll never have to think about us again."

"You do not know him too well," Javier said. "That is not how he operates. He has many hands in many cookie jars, all at the same time. His main client, whether it is Escobar or not, shouldn't concern you anymore. That is only one jar. You and Marilyn, unfortunately, are another one. He must attend to all jars, comprende? They are all of utmost importance."

"But we'd disappear, go so far away."

"The world is small, compadre. There is nowhere to hide. The Card, it is coming everywhere."

A lone tear dripped into my mouth, salty and sour. It was the moment I knew that there would be no happy ending. Even if I escaped then, somehow, somewhere Gable would catch up to me, the anticipation of death sure to kill me before he'd have the chance.

"So do it," I yelled. "Pull that trigger."

"If you insist," Javier said.

I chewed on my lip waiting for it. Drew some blood. Out of the corner of my eye, a hanging pan shimmered. I had to fight until I couldn't fight anymore. I couldn't just give in.

I made for the pan as Javier fired, narrowly missing me, the bullet whizzing by my cheek. It hit the sink, water exploding everywhere in a cascade of relief. A spray shot in our direction, drenching me and Javier. He lost focus and gave me a second to grip the pan and launch it at his face. A squeal erupted from him as it ricocheted off his forehead, drawing blood.

"Ah fuck," he yelled, as I crouched low. He got off another shot that hit something. I charged at him, catching his waist and bringing him down hard. As his body hit the floor, his bones seemed to shatter. He howled and got off another shot that burst the light. My eyes adjusted to the darkness. A body to the left of us slumped to the floor: Jack with the Nose coughing up blood.

"Jack," Georgie screamed, leaping up and rushing over to his friend.

I grappled at Javier's face, mashed his John Lennon glasses until it cut into his skin. He grabbed my hair and brought me back to my knees. We wrestled on the ground. Another bullet went off.

"No, no, no," I heard Georgie cry. A shadow darkened behind me as Georgie leaped on top of us.

"You fucker, you fucker," Georgie shouted. I didn't know who he was talking to, me or Javier, likely both of us. Fists were swinging all over the place. I couldn't get a handle on who I was pummeling. Javier was a bloody mess, the glasses slicing up his face. He emerged like a demon, teeth snapping, long fingernails slicing at my cheeks. Georgie and I were both going for his gun, Georgie looking possessed. My arm felt a burst of hurt as I saw he had dug his teeth in. I shook him off and bashed him with my elbow. He smiled a toothless smile and grabbed the pan on the floor. He swung hard and I ducked as Javier got knocked like the gong in the Gong Show. The gun fell from his hands. I dove and scooped it up, did the math in my head, and couldn't remember if it had two or three bullets left. Someone latched onto my leg and brought me to the floor again, my chin hitting the tiles, my tongue a burst of excruciating pain. I kicked backwards getting Georgie right between the eyes and then crawled away on my elbows. As I went to rise, a body flopped on top on me, light as a skeleton writhing around. I squirmed, clutching the gun as tightly as I could. Javier's stringy hair had covered his bloody face looking inhuman, a creature erupting from the depths of the Earth. Both his hands reached for the gun, squeezed to get off a shot. I lost another bullet. He went to squeeze off another, but then I felt another weight on top of me. Georgie had flopped on top of Javier and I was carrying them both on my back. With all my might, I shot to my feet throwing them both off of me. I spun around pointing the gun their way, expecting any surprise. I wouldn't waste my bullets on them. The window was open and since Javier had grabbed a butcher knife he intended to throw in my direction, I didn't want to take a chance on making it to the front door. He let the butcher's knife go with a cry as I leaped for the window, squeezed my body out as the knife bounced off the glass. I hung on from the sill, legs dangling. A one-story drop. Their bloody faces emerged at the window, ready to climb out too. I let go, praying I wouldn't break my legs, suspended in air. The sidewalk rushing up as I collided, limbs concaving like a marionette, splayed before a pack of old Chinese men smoking their cigarettes outside of a restaurant.

A black car had been parked, the driver's door opening. A man exited, his face obscured, sausage fingers reaching toward me that I hoped could help me up, but likely would end me for good.

42

Large hands grabbed me by the collar and dragged me into the black car.

The man propped me up at the wheel and ran to the passenger's side, swinging open the door. I rooted around in my pocket for the gun I stashed but he already had one in my face before I could get the chance. Spencer Tracy. Honestly, it would have either been him or Olivier. Other than that, Gable had no one left.

"Drive," Spencer Tracy ordered.

"Where?" I said, my hands on the steering wheel. I pulled out of the parking spot and onto the street.

"Card's office," he said. Of all the operatives, Spencer Tracy had the warmest face. Your friend's dad, incapable of causing harm. The man under the mask a different story.

"Is Marilyn there?" I asked.

"You need to be more concerned with yourself," Spencer Tracy said. "What was your plan, to run away? Where would you go?"

"Far. I told the same thing to Javier. Gable wouldn't have to worry. I'd never speak of the Card. It would be as if I didn't exist."

"He wouldn't give up Marilyn."

"So he has her?"

"I was just told to find you."

"What does he plan to do with me?"

"Whether it's an icing or a torture, it won't be pretty."

"You could say you never found me."

He gave a small laugh. "Then I'd be iced or tortured."

"What actually is his relationship with Marilyn?"

Spencer Tracy took a beat. "You didn't hear this from me." I shook my head like I had no idea who was speaking. "It's mutual. She loves him, he loves her, how it's always been since I started. They'd pretend they weren't a thing, but it was plain to see."

"She said she was gonna meet me so we can leave together. You don't know the relationship we had. If she loved Gable, she didn't love him anymore."

"Well." He scratched his chin with his free hand. "It don't matter. The Card employs many operatives not in masks. Only Gable knows who they are. Even if you would've gotten out of New York, one of them would've found you."

"Is this what you want?"

"Huh?"

"What you want out of life? Getting people their desires but also doing the bidding of a madman?"

"I don't think of it that way."

"How do you then?"

"Like a soldier in battle. Does what he's told. I do what I'm told."

"How long will it be before he turns on you too?"

A dent in the guy's armor. I saw him flinch. A fluttering of his left eye.

"I'm not a dope like you. I know my place at the Card."

"I guess I never did."

"No, you didn't."

We turned down Madison Avenue away from the thick of traffic. A few buses idling at their stops. The occasional pedestrian darting across the street. My day would end in an icing, no doubt. Gable having one final word with me before he did the deed himself. My parents hearing about it on the local news once my body would be found somewhere in the East River with the garbage. Ma convulsing in an eruption of tears. Pop staying stoic but giving in, his ticker unable to handle the shock. The destruction I'd bring forth, it was too damn pathetic to imagine.

"Nuh-uh," I said.

"What?" Spencer Tracy replied.

"Nuh-fuckin'-uh."

I slammed on the gas as the car barreled down Madison Avenue. The steering wheel spun through my fingers as I made a hard right.

"What the fuck are you doin–?"

Spencer Tracy didn't have time to finish his question because the car ran headfirst into a pole on the corner. I snapped forward into the steering wheel, banging my head but I defused the pain by throwing my arms across my face. Spencer Tracy wasn't so lucky.

He shot out of the seat because the dipshit wasn't

wearing a seatbelt. The force of the impact launching him straight out of the window and shattering broken glass all over the pavement. I wiped the blood from my eyes, not even checking to see what kind of damage I'd done to my own body. Passerby were collecting around Spencer Tracy's quivering body. The guy hadn't died, but was definitely in some kind of pain. They pointed at me, yelled for the police to be called, but I took off. I ran down a side street onto Park Avenue. I was close enough to the Card's offices. I had to know if Marilyn was being held there. If she loved Gable more than me. I couldn't believe that nonsense.

But when I passed the Card's offices, Police Line Tape had been put up around the scene. I'd forgotten Bette Davis was killed at the front steps that morning. With police milling about, no chance Gable was upstairs with Marilyn. I had no idea if there were other offices or where else they could be. But I didn't have time to question because Olivier was patrolling the scene. Our eyes locked as I took off down Park Avenue. I could hear him close behind. Catching up, grabbing the back of my shirt as he yanked me off the avenue.

43

"You idiot," Olivier said. "What are you doing here?"

I was stunned, expecting to be knocked out or beat up. He shook me in frustration.

"Why aren't you gone already?" he asked, and then finally let go.

"Marilyn. I came for Marilyn."

"There's no good hanging around here. Cops everywhere. Gable's been gone since this morning. After Bette..."

"Where is he?"

"I don't know. He called me at my hotel. Said to go after you."

"And now that you have me?"

I was prepared to bring out the gun I'd taken from Georgie's and ice him if need be. But Olivier always was an odd guy, unlike the rest.

"I'm supposed to ice you."

"Spencer Tracy was bringing me to the Card's

office," I said. "But I crashed the car and put him through the windshield."

"He obviously didn't get the updated memo."

"I can't go anywhere without Marilyn."

"Save yourself," he said, grabbing me by the collar as if he was speaking into a mirror. I knew he wanted out of the Card more than anything. But this was his lot in life. He started the Card with Gable and therefore the only way he'd ever be free was if it came to an end. Through his masked eyes, I could visualize his pain, his purgatory.

"We were supposed to meet on a ferry and sail away," I said. "Start a new life."

His head hung low. "There are no new lives for us."

"I'm seeing that."

"Does he have her? Please, you have to tell me. Does she want to leave him?"

"I don't know these things. Being at the international office, I'm out of the fold."

"She can't love him."

"Love him? No, I do not think so."

"But Spencer Tracy said–"

"Spencer Tracy is a fool with two marbles knocking around his head in lieu of a brain. Do not listen to him. You love her, yes. I understand this. I loved Katherine Hepburn, or Shelia, she had a real name. She had a fucking real name. I loved her and look where it got us. She was killed and I'm indentured. No chance. You have a chance."

"But if Marilyn's in trouble?"

"Then there is nothing you can do to save her. If Gable wants her, she is a slave too. But you, go on a ferry, sail the hell away, start a new life for yourself."

I started to cry.

"No, no," he said, his arm around me. "Cry once you are free. You do not have the luxury now."

"I'll never forgive myself for leaving her. It'll eat at me."

"When is the last ferry?"

"Dusk."

He looked toward the sun, sinking between the tall buildings, shading the sky pink and purple, orange and blue.

"You do not have much more time," he said. "Maybe she is there, but if she isn't, you get on that boat, you do what all of us wish we could."

"Why are you helping me?"

He thought about this for a moment, breathed it in. "I have never killed someone, Errol."

"It's Jake," I said, shaking away that fake name, never wanting to hear it again.

"Jake, like I said, I have never taken a life. I have done wrongs. I am aware that I am not a good man. Good men wouldn't allow themselves to slip like I did. And it was so easy. Gable and I, fuck—he isn't actually Gable. Although he has morphed into someone I no longer can understand. We sought money. And who could blame us? We got a window into this world with our wine business. The ultra-rich. And what a life they led! The idea of spending thousands for a bottle of vino. Insane. The thrill when they obtained a bottle they had sought for too long. Gable, speaks of the power he holds. I felt it too. It was like a drug. And more money than I'd ever seen. That was just from wine. Once we transitioned into other desires, I fed off our success. But no one like him. I could tell it wasn't the money that mattered. Money is just an idea, it's paper. What he sought was what can't be bought. And it's more than power. It was the ability to be a thumb and have everyone under it: politicians, CEOs, celebrities. People with authority, clout, but he had them wanting him, needing him like an addict. Susceptible to blackmail. Not that I've ever seen him stoop to the level, but he could. And that fear kept them loyal, subservient. The people he's already collected, the collective power they hold, I can even envision what the future may hold for the Card. Bigger than nations, certainly with more capital, the ability to destroy anyone they pleased, a network of cells all fighting for the same purpose. If I wasn't so scared of the outcome, I'd be in absolute awe."

The sun hid behind the Chrysler Building, casting a shadow over Olivier, his face in darkness.

"I'm a part of the machine whether I like it or not. And I'm mortified by what we've done, but I'm equally amazed. But you, run away if you can. Get a new face, new identity, never speak of Errol Flynn, never wish for anything again."

He turned his collar up and ducked into the shadows, blending in entirely until I couldn't see him at all.

44

WAITING FOR THE FERRY TO COME WAS TORTURE
since Marilyn hadn't shown yet.

If I missed this one, another wouldn't arrive until
tomorrow. I'd be iced by then. Once I heard it churn
through the waters, I knew I had to let her go. I bought
my ticket and got on. The ferry would head up the
Hudson and from there I'd hitch my way to Canada. I
didn't have much cash but I had a gun. I wouldn't use it,
but I would pretend to if I got into trouble. I was done
killing.

The ferry left the dock, the air with the tang of salt,
of hope. I let myself cry one last time for her as
Manhattan receded away. The tall buildings becoming
tiny blurs before vanishing. I stayed on deck making
sure I assessed every passenger. Spencer Tracy said that
Gable employed regular citizens now, anyone sent to ice
me. At least up top, it would make a scene.

The sun tucked itself into the waters, melted like
rainbow sherbet. Its warmth left my body. The cold air
snapped, bitter in my lungs. The rocking of the ferry

made me have to piss, the bathroom down below. I held out for as long as I could but wouldn't make it to the end of the line. Downstairs less crowded than above. There were some benches with someone asleep against the window. An old man stirring his paper cup of coffee.

As I went to open the bathroom door, a gun cocked at the back of my head. I was sloppy, deserving this fate. Maybe I wished for it to come because I couldn't go on my own without her. No chance it was Spencer Tracy after the car wreck. Javier and Georgie too beat up. Olivier surprisingly on my side. The old man stirring his cup of coffee? The guy fake snoozing on the bench? Or had Gable decided to take care of me himself?

A gloved hand reached out and opened the bathroom door, nudged me inside. Flipped on the light switch that crackled and buzzed. In the mirror, I conjured Gable, slicked-black hair and a mustache, fitted suit and the last bullet I'd see.

But the mirror didn't reveal the Boss like it should have, my assassin more beautiful. Blonde hair surrounding her face in a curly halo. The same white dress cut low at the neck she'd been in since the morning. Her masked lips struggling with what to say. I spoke first to make it easier for her.

"He sent you?"

She gave a precise nod, as if I should understand. But I couldn't. We were on the ferry, free. She didn't need him. She shouldn't need him. But like a parasite he had infiltrated. Reasoning with her would be an impossibility.

"You love him?"

Her eye hole watering, far from false tears. She

loved me but love wasn't enough. Not when fear held more power.

"I don't know what love is," she said. "You have to learn, right? It has to be taught somehow."

She'd dropped her cutesy-Marilyn voice, limply holding the gun. Could I grab it quick, force her to shoot at the wall? Or turn it back on her? Nothing about her deception should have surprised me.

"I could teach you," I said, with a goofy shrug. I cracked a smile and thought I saw her do the same under the mask, where reality lay.

"You know he'll ice me if I don't ice you," she said, the word *ice* causing a chill, a chattering of teeth.

"In Canada? At the other end of the world? There has to be a place he can't find us."

"There isn't."

"Spencer Tracy told me he's got regular people on his payroll."

"The old man drinking coffee," she said, swallowing. "The other guy sleeping. They are monitoring to make sure no one comes in here. An Out of Order sign already put up. We're expanding," she said, switching back to Marilyn. "I've been a part of the Card for years and to see where we are now, all I've worked to help get us to this place..."

"So this is what you wished for?"

"As a little girl on the streets, no one to trust, I wished just to be safe. With you, we'll never be safe. You know this. Always looking over our shoulders. I can't live like that anymore. When I joined the Card, I promised I'd never live that way again. Errol, please understand."

"It's Jake. Jake Barnum. You know my name."

"Okay, Jake, I can understand that."

"Lose the mask, come with me," I said, reaching out my hand. "I'll protect you. Every day. Someone will have to kill me to get to you."

She sucked in a saliva bubble.

"Don't make this harder–"

"I'm gonna make this as hard as I can for you. Because you don't wanna do it. I can see it in your hesitation. You fucking love me, girl. Just as much as I care for you. And you know that you'll replay this over and over for the rest of your life if you pull the trigger."

"Errol..."

"Jake! It's fucking, Jake! You fucking call me who I am. Jake is the guy you loved, Errol nothing more than rubber."

"Shut up, let me do this."

"And my baby, my goddamn baby. You okay with icing his father? We could have a family. You grew up an orphan, you know what it's like to have a hole in your heart. Don't destroy our family."

"Jake, the baby is why..."

"Why what?"

"Why you have to die. It's yours, it's definitely yours." She was sweating so profusely the mask was beginning to unstick. "And Gable couldn't have that. He's always wanted me all to himself. The child will have a family, don't you see?"

"It's just lies. It won't last forever."

"Don't say that," she said, shaking her head back and forth like a mental patient.

"He'll turn on you like he will to everyone else. And he already has a family, you're a side-piece."

"He said he'll leave his wife eventually."

"You fool, Marilyn. You want to believe him so bad you'll convince yourself anything. My promise is a guarantee."

"So what's the solution? We'll be poor, scraping by and unable sleep for fear of being iced in the night. I told you I *won't* live like that."

"I'm not worth it?"

"No, *I'm* worth it. I made a promise at a very early age to look out for only myself. Because no one ever gave me reason to think otherwise."

I stepped toward her. "I'm giving you reason. We can figure this out. Find happiness. Shit, we deserve it."

"Step back, Jake." She wiggled the gun. "I'll pull the trigger."

"Do it. Do it. Do it."

"Jake, move away—"

"I'm in your face, baby, close like we've always been." My lips hovered over hers, electricity sparking. "You ice me while looking right in these eyes that love and worship you like no one else, even Gable ever would."

"Please, Jake..."

"I won't make it easy for you. I can't."

My tongue licked at hers, tasted her desperation.

"Please..."

"You didn't want to fall for me, but you did, fucking hard. Say it."

"Jake..."

"Say what I mean to you. I'll haunt your dreams if you ice me. I'll never let you go."

"Jake!" she screamed. The gun poked my guts.

"He's not God," I said, blowing into her ear. "And

he's not the devil either. Just a puny human. You don't owe him."

"You're not listening..."

"I'm all fucking ears, baby. I'll listen to you till we're old and crumbling. I'll fight for us. You know I will." I cupped her face in my hands. "Take off the Marilyn mask."

"Don't touch..."

I started to unstick it, the chin first, the cheeks unpeeling.

"Stop..."

"We'll leave it in the fucking garbage. We'll never watch an old movie again. We'll live in the present."

"Jake, stop..."

"Sssshhh, it's all right, I got you. We got this."

The nose became unglued as the mask hung soggy. I was weeping, blurring my vision.

"Tell me who you are," I said.

"I can't."

"Your real name, that little girl deep down who just wanted a home. She's not Marilyn."

"She doesn't exist."

"She always has."

I went to lift the mask over her eyes to see her true self. Her mouth had turned down to a dangling frown but I imagined it a beaming smile, scars and all.

"I made her disappear," she said, jamming the gun farther into my gut. I reached down to move it away, clasped my hands around the cold metal. The mask hung from one spot on her forehead, leaving a distorted Marilyn staring back.

"It's okay," I said. "Tell me your name. Whisper it. He'll never know. He'll never fucking know."

"I was destined to be Marilyn when I was born. My real name so close anyway, as if it was meant to be. But I can't say it out loud. I won't."

"You can, it'll be freeing. It was for me. Jake Barnum, who I've always fucking been. Jake Barnum who loves you so much. Say yours."

Her cheeks flushed. Lips parted as she revealed her true self, but I couldn't hear from the sound of the gun firing. The bullet heavy like a cannonball. I doubled back, picking organs out of my body, holding guts in my hands. I sunk to the ground, lay against the dirty bathroom floor. Her high heels stepped over me. She fixed her Marilyn mask, smoothing it down over her nose and chin.

I coughed up a chunk of blood into my fist. She bent over me like a hovering angel, gave one last tear-filled red kiss before rising to her feet and sticking the gun between my eyes.

"It's Norma," she said, before pulling the trigger.

AN EDGE-OF-YOUR-SEAT ACTION WHERE MORALS AREN'T AS BLACK AND WHITE AS WAS ONCE THOUGHT.

J.D. Storm is an ex-Army sniper, discharged after losing an eye in battle. Finally finding work at the illusive Desire Card —an unsavory organization that promises *"any wish fulfilled for the right price"*—he heaves a sigh of relief. But when those wishes become too immoral, J.D. quickly finds out that no one reneges on the boss, a powerful and eccentric madman known only as Clark Gable because of the realistic mask he wears, without paying a hefty price.

On the run, J.D. begins a white-knuckle cat-and-mouse chase that takes him northwest where he hides out with a former girlfriend and tries to scrounge up enough cash to flee the country. But with every second that passes by, Gable's other masked operatives are closing in.

Soon, J.D. discovers just how widespread the organization's contacts are—no longer knowing who he can trust. Rather than running, J.D. decides that his best shot is to take out the head of the snake. After all, the hunted must become the hunter if he has any hope of surviving.

Ingeniously plotted and filled with twists and turns, *Prey No More* follows those indebted to this sinister organization— where the ultimate price is the cost of one's soul.

"Part international thriller, part down and dirty heist tale, Prey No More is a lightning-fast novel about human desire and the survival instinct."

—Scott Adlerberg, author of *Graveyard Love* and *Jack Waters*.

AVAILABLE JULY 2022

ABOUT THE AUTHOR

Lee Matthew Goldberg is the author of eight novels including *The Ancestor* and *The Mentor* and the YA series *Runaway Train*. His books are in various stages of development for film and TV off of his original scripts. He has been published in multiple languages and nominated for the Prix du Polar. *Stalker Stalked* will be out in Fall '21. After graduating with an MFA from the New School, his writing has also appeared as a contributor in *Pipeline Artists, LitHub, The Los Angeles Review of Books, The Millions, Vol. 1 Brooklyn, LitReactor, The Big Idea, Monkeybicycle, Fiction Writers Review, Cagibi, Necessary Fiction, Hypertext, If My Book, Past Ten*, the anthology *Dirty Boulevard, The Montreal Review, The Adirondack Review, The New Plains Review, Maudlin House, Underwood Press*, and others. His pilots and screenplays have been finalists in *Script Pipeline, Book Pipeline, Stage 32, We Screenplay*, the *New York Screenplay, Screencraft*, and the *Hollywood Screenplay* contests. He is the co-curator of *The Guerrilla Lit Reading Series* and lives in New York City. Follow him at LeeMatthewGoldberg.com.

CPSIA information can be obtained
at www.ICGtesting.com
Printed in the USA
LVHW032158210522
719247LV00008B/69

9 781685 490850